TRUE BEGINNINGS

The Lost and Found Series

Book Three

Amanda Mackey

TRUE BEGINNINGS

Limitless Publishing, LLC
Kailua, HI 96734
www.limitlesspublishing.com

Formatting: Limitless Publishing

ISBN-13: 978-1-64034-429-7
ISBN-10: 1-64034-429-2

Chapter One

Viper

It had stolen me. War. Battle. The thrill of being in mortal combat and danger. Not knowing one moment to the next whether I'd still be breathing. Walking. Talking.

I hated that I loved it. Like a strange sickness, it shackled its hooks into my psyche and refused to let go.

Even now, slumped over my wooden kitchen table drinking harsh black coffee at three a.m. because war-induced insomnia wouldn't let me settle for too long, my right leg jiggled nervously, as if in anticipation of the next phone call. The next mission. I had all my gear packed and ready to go at a second's notice, my brain never truly relaxing into civilian mode.

Weeks had passed since my best friend Declan Harding traded his life for his girlfriend, Mac's. She'd been taken from University Hospital at gunpoint, where she worked as a nurse and held hostage in a bid to lure Dec straight to the enemy. Live bait. It had worked too. But there had been no way in hell I was letting him die by the very scumbags we hunted in battle. Not on my watch. I'd witnessed our buddy Reno dying while we watched helplessly, and I would gladly sacrifice myself before letting anything happen to my brother from another mother.

It just so happened that the outcome had been favorable, and even though he still had deep issues which he dealt with daily, Mac held him up good and proper. I envied what they had. A connection so strong, they could literally sense when the other entered a room before actually seeing them. A need to support the other so strongly, it surpassed all else. They'd found what most people wanted, and every day I could see that bond grow even stronger. He needed her and she needed him. So simple. Together they could overcome anything.

Outwards, I appeared normal, even to those closest to me. Even Dec. But the visions and constant torment between good and evil never really abated. I existed on autopilot. Smiling when required. Eating. Sleeping on and off when the nightmares allowed it.

Every time I walked down the street, past regular folk, I wondered if they could see through my façade. They all went about their daily lives, ensconced in trivial drama, feeling as if the weight of the world lived on their shoulders. Whining about their favorite television show ending, boyfriend or girlfriend drama, missing the bus. I listened closely to strangers' chatter. How they made mountains out of molehills. Did they really understand the gravity of true stress? Perhaps a small minority with life-threatening illnesses or loss of loved ones. Those who battled with abuse and alcoholism. Mental illness. That small percentage would understand my pain. The rest had no idea what it was like to stare into the eyes of a friend and comrade while his throat was slit, watching the fear in his eyes. The pleading to help, all the while knowing you can't. Trying to calm young men with limbs blown off while trying to survive yourself. Mothers and children gunned down seconds before you can reach them. Not to mention babies being left amongst rubble of bombed villages. Some dead, others dirty, hungry and parentless. No. I'd say most people had no fucking idea what true fear meant. So it pissed me off big time to live in a society where everyone sweated the small stuff…sometimes the biggest drama being the internet being cut off.

I'd been on medication way too long and probably would be for the rest of my life, but after the last assignment of saving Dec and Mac, I wondered if the two small tablets were cutting it anymore. Seeing my best friend walk to his death cut me to the bone and shifted something further in my already messed up head. That's why I only ever averaged about four hours' sleep a night before I woke to a vision. One of the thousands my head had tried to process over the years.

Doctors had put me on the highest dose of anti-depressants possible, so with them becoming less effective, the only way to slake my thirst for the adrenalin kick of combat was to wait for the call to go on another mission. It was truly fucked up, because war had screwed me up in the first place and now I needed it to survive.

Downing the last of my black coffee, I spied my cell on the table where I'd haphazardly thrown it earlier. I searched for Dec's number, knowing he'd be curled up next to Mac, asleep. His dreams had abated somewhat, although not altogether, but at least he had the comfort of a warm, female body to distract him. I had nothing. Not anymore. Another thing war had stolen from me.

My finger hovered over his number. Did I let my friend know just how much his rescue had tipped me into the dark zone, or did I continue to act like I had my shit together?

The silence had me overthinking things. I honed my hearing in to any sound which might allow me to focus on something other than my warped deliberations, but the house remained silent.

Standing and placing my cup in the sink, I nabbed my keys from the kitchen counter and stalked to the front door, stopping to throw on my Nike running shoes.

It didn't matter that most people were tucked away in bed, fast asleep. It certainly didn't matter about the pitch black of night. It provided me with a certain amount of comfort. Quiet. Solitude. I needed to run. Movement helped to silence my mind. To soothe the endless noise. Visions only reserved for enlisted men and women and retired veterans.

Under the canopy of a starlit canvas, I took off. Feeling the rough surface of the road, I kept close to the curb in case of any traffic, although at such an ungodly hour, it would be minimal. I let the street lamps guide me. Past silent, parked suburban cars and houses, focusing on each step, allowing it to ground me.

My disquiet ebbed back to a more manageable level as my lungs drank in the crisp air.

Unsure of how long I pushed on, not caring to look at my watch, I startled when a white Jeep Cherokee pulled up alongside me and the driver's window slid down. I pivoted my head to face Mac's annoying friend Char, who smiled at me as if she were merely pulling up for a middle of the night chat. She was in her scrubs, so it became obvious her shift at the hospital had ended. I was in no mood for idle chitchat. Especially with her. For some reason, she made my snarky side rise into being.

"Hey there! You always go running in the middle of the night?" she asked, keeping her vehicle in pace with me, glancing backward and forward to the road and then at me again.

I just wanted a peaceful jog. To rid the excess thoughts plaguing me. To exhaust myself so that I might actually get some sleep. Fate obviously had other ideas. I didn't respond for a minute as I breathed heavily, attempting to not fire back at her like I wanted to. She didn't appear fazed by my silence and the white vehicle kept pace.

Finally glancing at my watch, I answered while clenching my jaw to restrain myself from telling her to get lost. "It's three thirty a.m. It's far from the middle. It's practically morning." I don't know what sparked the need to goad her, but for some reason, the fiery red hair and green eyes made me uncomfortable, and I had never figured out why.

I certainly didn't feel like company. My therapeutic jog was being interrupted. Wishing she'd hit the gas and move along, I faced forward again and upped my pace slightly, feeling the lactic acid burn in my calf muscles.

"Do you need a ride somewhere?" Silly question.

Keeping my eyes on the approaching intersection, I huffed out, "Do I look like I'm in need of assistance to you?"

Would she take the hint? Doubtful.

With her SUV lolling beside me, I stopped. She braked, seeing me take pause, so I took two long strides to her open window and with a tone I hoped would scare her off, I barked out, "Do you need something? Cause if you just want a friendly chat, I suggest you catch up with Mac when she wakes up. I'm sure she has all the time you need."

Her face betrayed her, showing a flash of annoyance. Good.

"Man, you truly don't like people, do you? I've just finished work and saw you running at an ungodly hour, and wondered if you needed to be taken somewhere. I can see I shouldn't have bothered."

A few curls of her red hair hung loose around her face. If I wasn't such an ass, I would have thought her attractive with her sensational green eyes.

Not knowing what to say, I changed the subject.

"I thought you'd switched to days, anyway?"

Still miffed, she gripped the wheel, no doubt wishing it were my head. "Not that it's any of your business, but I pulled an extra shift for another nurse. And in response to your earlier, snarky comment, I wasn't after some deep, meaningful chat. I'll be sure to go to Mac for that. While I'm at it, I'll tell her what a jerk you are."

With that, she pressed on the gas and left me with exhaust fumes and an unusual grin on my face. Damn. The woman had balls. I'd give her that.

Chapter Two

Char

What an arrogant prick! So much for trying to be nice. The guy had given me grief ever since turning up at the hospital with Harley when Mac had been kidnapped. He hated me then and he hated me now. I don't know what I'd done to flick his *asshole* switch, but it only appeared to be aimed at me. Screw him. Even if he was a hotter than hell dick, it would be in my best interests if I steered clear of him. Problem with that was, I had a misguided attraction to the wrong types of men. I saw them as a challenge. After all the no-hopers I'd dated since high school, you'd think I'd steer clear of that type, but I wanted what I wanted. Viper proved no different.

Stepping on the foot pedal after pulling a double shift, I just needed to get home and sleep. After changing to day shift with Mac, I hadn't pulled a double in a while, and if I could prevent it, I wouldn't be doing it again. My feet had gone numb and my leg muscles had tightened to the point of pain.

I loved my job, but it didn't agree with me when I'd worked almost twenty-four hours straight.

After turning into my apartment complex and parking in my single car garage, I literally stumbled through the small kitchen and living areas, dumping my bag on the couch on my way down the hallway.

Thoughts flicked back to the douchebag I'd encountered not even ten minutes earlier. What was his problem with me? My looks were above average. I wasn't short at five foot eight. My patients and colleagues all liked me. Sure, I spoke it as I saw it, but shit, even Mac's boyfriend Dec liked me.

Pushing open my bedroom door, the darkened room soothed me. I did a quick strip and climbed into bed naked, too exhausted to find a tank and sleep shorts.

My last coherent thought before succumbing to oblivion was, *You still want to play the angry soldier card with me, Viper? Game on!*

***

Stirring reluctantly in my dark surroundings, it took a minute to get my bearings. My block out curtains made it hard to determine what time of the day it was. I'd been immersed in an idiotic dream about a tall, blond soldier with a buzz cut. In the world of make believe he'd been more humane and friendly toward me. In fact, way too friendly. My groin tingled as snippets of hot kisses and urgent touches broke through my haze. Pfft. As if. That was as likely to happen as a trip to Mars in my lifetime.

I needed to get those images out of my head right now.

A familiar ringtone sounded from the living area. My horse whinny that everyone hated, especially when I had it at full volume like I did now.

Rising soberly, not caring I had no clothes on, I hurried down the hallway to retrieve it before it went to the message bank. Praying it wasn't the hospital, relief had me sag into a chair after spying the caller.

"Hey, Mac. I thought you were working today."

"Hello to you too! I'm at work. I'm on a break."

Eying the time as three p.m. in the afternoon, I asked, "What's up? How's Mrs. Sullivan in room 190?"

"She's had another turn. Tests came back as an aneurysm in the brain. We've admitted her for now under observation. Because of her age, surgical clipping may be too risky."

"What size are we looking at?"

"It's small and less than a quarter inch, so Doctor Atkins thinks observation is best at this time."

"Okay, well, I'll be back in the morning. How's that hunk of a man of yours? Have his meds for PTSD fully kicked in yet?"

"He's doing much better. Still having a few nightmares, but nothing like he was. His moods have stabilized."

"Pfft. Can't say the same for his jerk-wad of a friend." I said it more to myself than to Mac, but it was out and I knew she wouldn't let it go.

"Who? Viper? You've seen him?" We'd spoken previously about how striking I thought the guy was, but each time he opened his mouth, my opinion of him went down that little bit more. Since Mac's rescue, I'd only run into him a couple of times and we'd barely said two words to each other, last night excluded.

"You could say that." My pause on how to continue and whether I should paint the guy in a better light gave Mac the opening to speak.

"Well? Are you going to tell me? I have about two minutes of my break left."

Deciding not to sugar-coat it, I held nothing back. "Your boyfriend's military buddy is a shit-eating, good for nothing piece of dog crap with no personality whatsoever."

Mac chuckled through the line.

"Oh, you think it's funny, do you?"

"Yeah. I actually do." She laughed harder.

Hearing a name paged through the line, Mac suddenly added, "That's me. I gotta run. I'll call by after work." She ended the call. She freaking ended the call before I could give her a snarky comment about her finding my opinion of Viper funny.

Throwing my head back into the chair, I balked. "Everyone seems to think the sun shines out of Mr. Military's butt. Pfft. They need their heads read."

***

Two and a half hours later I listened to Mac's beefy Mustang pull into the visitors' parking bay two apartments down. There was no other car in our complex that sounded quite like hers. For a pretty blonde nurse, the car was the exact opposite of her. Masculine. Fast. Powerful. Yet I couldn't imagine her driving anything else. The girl had spunk, like her car, and they kind of fit together nicely.

I personally preferred my SUV with all its space. Plus, God forbid I ever got into an accident, I liked the idea of having something substantial around me. Being on my own, if I wanted to pack up and head away for a couple of days, I could do so comfortably.

A soft knock sounded on my front door. I jumped off the sofa where I'd been a vegetable for the latter part of the afternoon and threw open the door.

Mac beamed as she pushed past me with a large coffee in each hand.

"Got your favorite. Double shot, skinny cappuccino."

I could have kissed her. She knew when I needed caffeine, and with my epic shift at work and then running into hot shit for brains, my energy was at an all-time low.

Shutting the door and taking the coffee she held out, I swigged it before answering. Feeling the burn but not caring, I smiled at my savior. "You're truly a lifesaver. I need two or three of these babies after the last twenty-four hours."

"Come. Sit. Tell me all about it." Her eyes gleamed as she beat me to the sofa.

"Well, you know about Mrs. Sullivan…"

"You know that's not what I meant. Viper! Tell

me why Viper has you so riled up?"

The sly smile on her face only grew wider. For some reason, Mac was enjoying the fact that a guy had me knotted up.

"You mean you haven't noticed how he treats me like garbage?" She'd have to be blind not to have seen or heard his responses to me.

"Yeah, but it's never bothered you this much. From your insanely colorful depiction on the phone earlier, something epic must have happened. Spill!"

Retelling the events of my trip home, I made sure she knew just how cool Viper's behavior toward me had been. I wasn't one to sugarcoat things. Especially with my best friend. She could do what she wanted with my brutal honesty.

Mac let me rant and get it all off my chest without interrupting, which I was grateful for because once I got started, I let loose.

"So you see why I'm so annoyed?" I puffed the words out, exhausted.

She wore a frown and her eyes showed a small glimmer of confusion. "I do know he was burned by a woman a while ago. The house he lives in was meant to be their home. She left. I guess it's not easy being the partner of a military soldier who's away on missions so much. They come back from war…different."

Watching Mac look to the ground while fiddling with the sofa cushion, I asked, "You worried Dec is going to go on another assignment? That he may not…you know…return?"

Her eyes lifted to mine and in them, I saw the truth.

"Yeah. If he decided to go, I don't think I'd sleep a wink until he came home. He's cheated death way too many times. Eventually, his luck has to run out."

I'd been so happy to see her with a guy who treated her like a queen, I hadn't considered her insecurities. After her ex, Nick, who had been almost non-existent in the relationship, Mac deserved someone who put her first. Still, I'd hate to see her hurt again and have to pick up the pieces.

"Maybe he'll decide not to go if it comes down to it. He has you now. Perhaps that's enough. Perhaps you're enough. He'd need a full medical anyway, and given his recent mental meltdown, my guess is they'd deem him unfit."

She smiled with only mild enthusiasm. "Maybe. Anyway, enough of the dreary talk. You up for going out for a bit tonight, or are you still recovering from the double you pulled?"

Ugh. The thought of getting dressed up and leaving the comfort of my apartment was none too thrilling, but when had I last gone out and enjoyed myself? And with Mac?

Deciding to ignore my bone-weary fatigue, I asked, "You driving?"

"Sure."

Checking the time, it was fife fifty p.m. I hadn't eaten dinner. I truly just wanted a hot shower and then bed, but Mac very rarely offered, so I put my own needs aside.

"I'll go for a couple of hours. And not somewhere flashy. Oh, and I'll need an hour or so to get ready."

Mac's cheeks pulled up into a generous smile. "Great! I'll be back at seven." Her gaze drew downwards and then back up as if she were assessing me. "Eat something too. You're pale and drawn in the face."

I wanted to scream at her that it probably had something to do with the fact that in the last day I'd had about ten coffees and a soggy veggie sandwich because I'd been run off my feet, but I let my bitchiness recede so that should I need to use it on Viper at a later date, it would be at full capacity.

After Mac left, I cursed the fact that I'd agreed to go out so easily. My feet still ached. My whole body sagged with exhaustion. But my friend had been through a major ordeal when she'd been kidnapped and thought she would die. Then she'd had to deal with Dec's full memory return and the PTSD which had come with it.

No. I'd grab some food, an energy drink, and a scalding shower, and I'd be good to go.

Chapter Three

Viper

"She said what?" I laughed as Dec vividly described what Char had called me. It should have angered me, but for some strange reason, it didn't. If anything, I found it amusing.

"You really pissed her off, man."

I heard him let out a loud breath into the phone. "Why are you such a dick to her, anyway? You like her or something?"

"Fuck that shit! You know me better than that after Sandy took off. I'm not looking for another needy female who can't handle my job. Besides, she's not my type."

"Oh, please! She's exactly your type. She gives as good as she gets. You should cut her some slack and be nice. She's Mac's best friend, so you'll be seeing a lot more of her."

I tried not to focus on that. The woman would have my balls if and when I saw her again. That much I was sure of.

"So, you want to go out for a bit tonight?"

Repeating his question, I asked, "You want to go out? Tonight?" Normally it was me asking Dec, not the other way around. He rarely instigated going to clubs unless it was work related.

"Sure. Mac and Char are going into town for a bit, and while she didn't ask me to go directly, I thought I'd hang in the background. Make sure she's okay."

"In other words, you want to spy on her. Come on, man, that's low, even for you. Don't you trust her?"

"I trust Mac. It's other assholes I don't trust. She does happen to be one of the hottest women in Ann Arbor."

I had to mentally agree. She had looks other females might be jealous of, but I didn't feel like tagging along on some stakeout.

I took pause, squeezing my eyes shut, trying to find the will to go. A certain redhead would be there and that could only mean disaster.

Dec chimed in, "You don't even have to take any money. My treat for drinks."

"Oh, you really are trying to bribe me. Look, as nice as the offer is, I really don't feel like getting slapped across the face and kneed in the groin by Char."

He roared at that remark, damn him. He was enjoying this too much. After composing himself, he asked, "Please? You can remain in the background like me. They won't even know we're there. I promise."

Dec didn't beg very often, but I could hear it in

his voice. If I didn't go, he wouldn't either, and then he would blame himself if anything happened to Mac. God. Did I really have a choice?

"Fine. You win, but I'm not staying long." I knew that would probably end up being a big, fat lie because once I got there and had a drink or two, I'd loosen up and get into the spirit of things. Maybe it's what I needed to help me settle.

"Thanks, bro. I mean it. Pick you up in an hour."

Ending the call, I strode into my bedroom to shower and pick out a shirt and some long pants to wear. He owed me big time. Not only for saving his ass but for losing mine tonight to a sassy redhead.

***

The music pumped so hard, I almost felt the walls jumping inside the club, Rave. Being early, we could move around freely and see plenty of spare tables and chairs. Heading to the bar first, Dec ordered two beers.

"Let's sit upstairs," he offered.

Agreeing that we were less likely to be noticed up there, I followed him. Last time we'd been here, Mac and Char had spent a good portion of the night dancing, so I hoped they'd do the same tonight so we could remain unnoticed.

Upstairs there were only a few people scattered around, so we found a spot near the balcony, but far enough away that we wouldn't be spotted unless we stood and leaned against the railing.

Downing some of my beer, deciding to just chill and be more in the moment, I pushed the niggling voices in my head back into the darkness.

"You seem distant." Dec could read me well. I didn't want to tell him about my inability to sleep more than four hours a night or the need to go into battle again. He thought I was handling my PTSD. I had been up until I'd had to save his ass.

Shrugging, I began to peel the label off the front of the bottle. "Just not sleeping lately, that's all."

Unable to look at him, I noted the pause. His appraisal. A weighted stare that I could feel rather than see.

"Hey." A hand on my arm. "Are you okay? I mean, you're not still rattled about your run in with Char, are you?"

As if a woman could make me feel hungry to maim something, or the need to pound my skull into a wall in order to try and erase images upon images of gore. No. War had done it. War would continue to do it, even if I never went into battle again. No meds could erase the past. Unlike Dec, who had been given that luxury for a while, my internal video recorder would continue on replay till the day I took my last breath.

"You think I care about what she thinks of me? I couldn't give two shits one way or the other." A seed of doubt popped through the muck but then disappeared quickly.

Finally glancing up, I found my friend's forehead creased with worry. He had enough of his own fucked up past to deal with. He didn't need my burdens too.

"I'm good. Truly. Just tired." Glancing toward the metal railing beside us, I asked, "You want to see if your girl's here yet?"

At the mention of his girl, he grinned. She'd stolen his heart. No doubt about it. After Trudy stomped all over it by screwing Reno, he was overdue for happiness.

Rising, after placing his beer on the table, he angled toward the railing, casually scanning the room below. He remained in shadow so as to be inconspicuous. I kinda hoped the girls had changed their minds about coming and then we could have another beer and head home.

Didn't look like that was happening though, as I watched Dec hone in on something below. His hand on the railing gripped tightly and his muscles flexed. Bingo. His woman had arrived. Which meant…ah, hell. I was dead meat.

Chapter Four

Char

Yawning as we entered the club, I already wanted to leave. My feet were hurting from the heels Mac had insisted I wear, and I pulled at the hem of the too short dress. God, I looked like shark bait.

Normally, I would have been all for dressing this way, but with fatigue threatening to drop me like a fly, I seriously had hoped I could turn up in my pajamas and comfortable slippers.

When had the tables turned? Mac appeared pumped and ready to party, and here I was, shoulders sagging and feet dragging. Most times it was the other way around.

I guess overdosing on work could do that to you.

"You want anything to drink?" Mac yelled over the loud music.

Did I? Not really, but one would help me relax. "Vodka and lemon," I called back, remembering our last time at the same club. Mac and Dec had been taking a break and she hadn't wanted to be here any more than I did tonight. Still, we'd danced our asses off, in between fighting off the jerk who'd become too handsy with Mac—right before Dec and Viper had saved the day and knocked the guy unconscious.

Man, Viper had looked hot that night.

Dragging my thoughts from the gutter as Mac handed me my drink, we found a table and sat, watching the handful of people on the dance floor.

A couple gyrated together, joined at the hips, not caring they were out of sync with the beat. They appeared in their own little world and I couldn't help the pang of jealousy I felt. Deep down I wanted someone to love who loved me back unconditionally, no matter how much I played the single, wild woman. Having my best friend hooked up with the man of her dreams and getting to see snippets of what it would be like, I yearned for the same. It had been two years since I'd last had a boyfriend. We'd been quite solid for the eighteen months before that, spending most nights together even though we lived separately. Derek had been a doctor at University Hospital, which is where we'd met. It turned out Dr. Derek had a hankering for pretty brunette nurses in the children's ward.

Lesson learned. Don't date anyone you work with. It had ended badly, and not long after, Derek had put in for a transfer, thank goodness or I would have ended up having to quit.

As it was, the humiliation of having everyone find out had been hard enough. With him gone though, and me not having to face the bitch he'd screwed within the grounds of the hospital, life had quickly returned to normal.

"Are you really okay?" Mac nudged me. "You haven't seemed yourself today. And don't give me the crap about being tired. I've seen you after pulling many double shifts, and you've never been like this." Her hand swept over me.

"Like what?" I tried to act dumb but didn't succeed.

"Oh, please. You forget who you're talking to. I know you. There's something else."

Watching the colored light play over her features as it morphed from red to blue, then green to yellow, I sighed, glancing at the couple on the dance floor, who were now exchanging saliva in a heated kiss. "I guess I just get lonely, you know? Seeing you and Dec together makes me wish I had a special someone."

Her features softened at my revelation. She reached out and placed her hand over mine, giving it a gentle squeeze. "I want that for you too. I'll have to talk to Dec and see if he can hook you up..." Realizing her mistake, she added, "Not Viper. I'm sure he's got other single friends."

"Have you ever seen him with anyone other than his bestie?"

I could tell Mac wanted to say yes, but she couldn't. "No. But that doesn't mean anything."

"Don't go there, Mac. I really don't need setting up." Wanting the conversation to end, I downed the rest of my drink and pulled her up. "Come on, as exhausted as I am, let's dance."

Feeling a little like the center of attention when

the other dancers, including the loved-up couple, left the floor, leaving only Mac and me, I tried not to be too worried. Normally I didn't mind being the center of attention, but I did feel like I was off my game.

Swinging my hips and letting my arms rise above my head, I closed my eyes and let the music wash over me.

I'm not sure how long we danced, but when my feet could take it no more, I motioned to Mac that I was going back to the table. She followed.

Glancing at my watch, I noticed we'd been lost to the music for a good half hour.

I could feel sweat in places I shouldn't. "I'm heading to the ladies to freshen up. You want to come?"

"Nah. I'm good. I'll get us another drink."

"Only one more for me. I want to be coherent at work tomorrow."

Watching her dig into her purse as she walked to the bar, I headed to the hallway that led to the bathrooms.

Inside, I relieved myself and washed my hands, glancing in the mirror. My makeup had all but slithered off with the sweat, leaving mascara and minimal lip gloss. I looked like I felt. Shattered.

With my shoulder bag still hanging across my torso, I dug into it and re-applied my lip gloss before exiting the bathroom. On my way down the hallway, I noticed the steps to the second level. I should have kept walking, but curiosity got the better of me. I'd never been upstairs and wanted to know what it looked like.

Scrambling up in my heels, I let my eyes adjust to the darker atmosphere, turning to scan the entire room. Another bar sat against one wall with tables and chairs scattered here and there. Finding the railing which overlooked the dance floor, I sucked in a breath when I found Dec and Viper sitting at a table, chatting idly. Hoping I wasn't spotted, I cringed as Viper's eyes left Harley's, and as he glanced to the right, his gaze stopped on me. His eyes widened slightly, but being the cool, calm, and collected soldier, he schooled the rest of his features well.

Not knowing what to do, I stood staring as if my feet were superglued to the floor. Dec, perhaps sensing Viper had fixated on something, turned and found me too. He grinned and started to rise from his seat.

Unable to handle facing his arrogant friend, I smiled and turned, hoping I could make it down the steps and into the crowd below before he caught up to me.

"Char!" Dec called, already halfway across the room.

Damn it! Couldn't he tell I didn't want to hang around?

"Wait!"

Gripping the handrail on the stairs, I stopped, turning slowly and plastering a fake smile on my face.

"Declan. Hi. What are you doing here? Mac didn't mention you were coming tonight. And speaking of such, why are you up here when she's downstairs?"

Had they had a fight she hadn't told me about? Or had they just not communicated to each other as to their activities tonight? Strange. They were inseparable.

Closing the gap, he stopped just short of me. Combing his hair with one hand while holding a beer with the other, I peered into his mocha eyes.

"Ahh, she doesn't actually know I'm here."

"Oh?"

He appeared slightly embarrassed. "I wanted to keep an eye on her. From a distance."

"You mean stalking!" I ground the words out.

"That's what Viper said too, but in light of everything that has gone down recently, I think my concern is warranted."

Blowing out a long breath, I let my eyes fall to his ample chest, visible against his fitted shirt, and then lower to the black jeans hugging his manly bits.

Eyes up, Char. He's taken, remember?

I had to hand it to my friend. She'd struck the jackpot as far as snagging a hottie went.

Shaking my head, I found Viper swigging on his beer while watching me. He looked even more amazing with a collared shirt and blue jeans on. The dim light prevented me from truly appreciating his green eyes, but I remembered them well.

Gah! I needed to stop ogling and get back to Mac.

"You girls want to join us up here? Now that you know we're here, it seems pointless to remain separate," Dec offered.

Not wanting to get any closer to Viper, I shook

my head. "Actually, we're probably heading home. I just needed to use the bathroom and decided to take a detour."

"Well, we were only staying a short time anyway." Glancing back to his friend, he motioned with his head to get up and join us.

Seeing the handsome soldier tense before rising, I turned my back on him, unable to withstand his piercing stare.

Huffing, I replied, "Fine. Whatever." I strode down the stairs, finding Mac still sitting at our table. Thankfully she was alone, which meant no douchebags had tried to hit on her, unlike last time.

I could feel and hear the two bulky guys behind me. They kept quiet as we approached Mac. She had her mouth open. Her eyes were fixated on her man.

"Dec? What are you doing here?" It seemed Viper was going to be ignored, as the girl only had eyes for one man.

Moving in toward her, Dec put his large hands under her armpits and lifted her from the chair, placing her on her feet but pulling her in close. "Angel. Don't be mad, but I just wanted to make sure you were okay."

Her eyebrow lifted but I could see her smirk. "You were spying on me?"

His thumb ran backward and forward across her cheek. "Not spying, per se. Just making sure you stayed safe." Leaning in, he brushed his lips over hers, making me look away. Each intimate gesture they exchanged proved awkward for me. I wondered if I was actually jealous of what Mac and

Dec shared. Normally I wasn't a jealous person, but when your best friend suddenly becomes deliriously happy and you're still running solo, you feel it in every corner of your lonely heart.

Viper cleared his throat behind me. "Ahem. We good to go now?"

Thank God, he'd interrupted. The last thing I felt like doing was watching any more kissing and canoodling.

I wanted to go home.

Mac and Dec broke apart, but not before I heard Dec ask Mac, "Stay at my apartment tonight?"

Nodding, she gave me a remorseful look.

Dec jumped in. "You good to give Char a lift home, man?" He clapped Viper on the shoulder.

What. The. Actual. Hell? No way.

Glaring at Viper and then Dec, I threw out, "Are you kidding me right now? Why can't I go home with you guys?"

"It's out of my way. Viper drives right past your place."

About to stomp my feet like a child and rant and rave about his idiotic idea, I was cut off by a deep, abrasive voice.

"Fuck, bro. I gotta agree with Char on this one. Are you serious?"

I shot him a death glare as well. It was like no one wanted to take me home. I suddenly felt like a fifth grader waiting until last to be chosen for the class baseball team.

Seizing Mac by the arm, I pulled her aside and gritted my teeth. "Seriously, girl. What is this? Why can't you just take me home? We came together.

You know how I feel about that jerk." I swung my arm backward, hoping I pointed at the right person.

"Keep your voice down. I think it would be good for you two to spend time together to sort out whatever it is between you."

"The only thing between us is a cold front, which is icing over further as we speak. I can't believe you'd do this to me."

In the background I vaguely heard Viper saying something similar to Dec, confirming my theory that he hated me.

"Look. It makes sense when he's driving right by your house. You don't have to talk to each other. He's not a total asshole, as much as you think he is. You both need to give each other a chance. Dec and I both want you to get on, and the only way for you both to do that is to start spending more time together."

God, she was being a bitch. "Ugh. I'm not standing here arguing with you. I'm ready to drop and need to get home into bed. If you want to ditch me, then fine. But you owe me, big time! See you tomorrow."

I didn't bother hugging her, I pivoted on my heels and walked over to Viper. My face was a mask of fury.

"Take me home. The sooner this is over with the better."

Storming past him, I headed to the door of the club.

Chapter Five

Viper

Yep. Definitely a spitfire. After briefly nodding at my friend, who'd set me up to endure the ride from hell, my eyes fell to the perky, globed ass of my nemesis as she flounced toward the club exit. The high heels accentuated her toned calves, and the skin-tight dress didn't leave much to the imagination.

My hormones were firing on all cylinders, and I had to adjust myself inconspicuously as I caught up to her.

So far she hadn't shoved my ass into a meat-grinder, but the ride home could prove to be a different story.

The frosty night air blasted me as I left the heat of the club. Patrons still queued up outside. It was only nine forty-five, so the night was still young. Some people didn't head out until eleven or midnight, and here I was already going home.

Upping my strides to catch up with Char, I

decided to appease her. The quick gait and extension of her spine told me to tread carefully. "I don't like this any more than you do, so let's just not speak, okay?"

Damn, she got under my skin.

Stopping, she spun on me, pushing at my chest with both hands. "How could you agree to drive me home? You know this was a setup, right?"

Truth was, I did know. Dec had spun me some bullshit about playing nice with Miss Wildcat and apologizing to her about the way I treated her. To hell with that. I didn't owe the woman anything. Even if the feel of her hands on me stirred dormant hormones to life.

Fire blazed in her eyes and all I wanted to do was push her up against the closest car and see how much hotter I could stoke the blistering sparks.

"Don't flatter yourself, Red. It was nothing more than my friend being too lazy to veer off his course and drop you home," I lied.

Before I could take my next breath, a hard slap to my face had me standing upright at full attention. The soldier in me came to life and the darkness stirred. The battle-hungry warrior saluted the sting, preparing for a showdown.

Gripping her wrist in a lightning-quick move, I spun us both around, pushing her into the light pole which stood between Char and a Humvee. My knee wedged her legs apart, the skimpy black dress riding up even higher.

Dropping my chin so I was right in her face, I sniffed in her scent as I took a deep breath to steady myself. I faltered only momentarily as the decadent fragrance wafted up my nostrils.

"You shouldn't have done that." I didn't know what else to say as her wild green eyes, slightly darker than my own, failed to look away. Adrenalin flowed, and from the feel of her chest rising and falling against my own, I'd say we stood on an even keel, her harsh breathing matching my own.

"Or what? You're going to strike me back? Huh? 'Cause you sure as hell seem as if you want to. From the moment we met, you look like you've wanted to punch me in the face. Go on then. Just do it, already."

Her breath with its alcohol-tinged aroma blew across my cheek. I had her trapped. She couldn't move. Did she think I would hit her? Or any woman, for that matter? Is that how I came across?

Fuck! I'd never laid a hand on a female. Ever. And I never would. The way her irises expanded and flicked with fear made me ease back a fraction. Not enough to let her go, though. Just enough to allay her fears that I was a crazy psycho who wanted to harm her.

"Is that what you think I want to do to you?"

Her sharp intake of air made me adjust my face slightly to assess her. The electricity, whether it be from the pole we leaned against or the energy crackling between us, rose exponentially.

My gaze lowered to her pouty mouth at the same time hers did to mine. Her pulse pounded under the weight of my hand around her wrist. It wouldn't take much to silence that sassy mouth.

My hormones roared, heat spreading from my thighs upward. I could feel my face inching closer to hers, the thrill of tasting her almost unbearable. My grip on her tightened as I attempted to cool my jets. In a war zone, I'd be charging at the enemy now, the sick thrill of the chase bleeding into every energized cell.

I could feel the mania just below the surface. Her lips plumped in preparation for my assault. I swear her nipples had hardened beneath the sheer fabric of the scrap of clothing she wore.

A car honked its horn and someone screamed out to get a room, breaking my lust-induced delirium.

Pushing off her, I stepped back, gaining some clarity. We were in the middle of a busy street, people walking past. Open to the public.

Whatever spell she'd had over me had well and truly been broken.

"The car's not too far," I growled. I couldn't look at her.

She didn't respond, simply followed me to my vehicle where I silently unlocked it and climbed in.

What the hell had happened back there? Jesus! This woman had me floundering. The sooner I got her out of my sight, the better. One minute I hated her, the next…

The second her door shut, I pressed the gas pedal and peeled out of the parking space. I could see her clutching her seatbelt out of the corner of my eye, but I didn't give a shit.

My heart was pumping so fast I could feel a tightness in my throat.

"Are you trying to get us killed? Could you slow down a bit?" she asked shrilly.

Hearing her intense plea, I eased off the gas

marginally. The last thing I needed was to get pulled over by the police. The two drinks I'd had might just put me over the alcohol limit.

Turing off the main road into the side streets, I decided I needed to find out where she lived. "What's your address?"

"You mean you don't know? Thought you'd have figured that one out before going past it."

Slamming my foot on the brake, I asked, "What?"

"My street. You've gone too far. You were supposed to take Wagner Road, and then Pleasant Lake Road."

I felt my blood pressure rising. Why had she let me keep going without telling me to turn? I scraped both hands over my face and into my hair, finally turning to face her.

Attitude clung to her again, after our near kiss earlier. Her arms lay folded across her chest.

I tried to ignore her bare legs and thighs glaring at me, even under the cloak of night. My soldier vision allowed me to virtually see in the dark. And damn, they were distracting me.

"Let me get this straight. You let me keep driving past your turnoff because, what? You were too pissed at me to mention it?" Placing my left hand back on the wheel, I gripped it for support.

"I thought you knew where I lived."

"And how would I know that?" Like I even cared.

"Dec or Mac could have told you."

"Yeah, well, they didn't, and you shouldn't assume anything." I lay a hidden meaning under the sentence. I wasn't sure if she picked up on it. I wanted her to know that no matter what she thought of me, I had reasons for being an ass.

"Just turn around and get me home. I'm over this night completely."

Facing the front, I huffed out, "You and me both," before indicating and turning around.

Dec was going to pay for this.

Chapter Six

Char

The next morning as I poured my steaming mug of coffee after stealing a break between patients, Mac walked into the staff cafeteria.

"Hey, girl. You made it home okay, I see."

Her cheery mood annoyed the hell out of me after she had placed me in the company of Satan last night.

"Don't *hey girl* me." I gave her the stink-eye, hoping she picked up on my annoyance.

Her smile wavered as she made her way to me.

Stirring my mug and throwing the spoon in the sink, I pushed past her to sit at a table.

"Okaaay…someone got out of the wrong side of the bed this morning." Following me, she sat opposite.

Burning my throat on the hot liquid, I hid my pain. "I got out on the right side of the bed, thank you very much."

She could work for my reasoning at being

pissed.

"So, I'm guessing you're still mad at me for allowing you to go home with Viper?"

Bingo. "I can't believe you let that happen. You know what a disaster the two of us are together, and last night was no different. Not to mention he nearly got me killed."

Her eyes widened in shock. "Shit. Are you okay? What happened?"

Wishing I could tell her Viper had harmed me physically so she'd see him for what he was, I pushed out a breath, knowing I had nothing. "I'm fine. He drives like a maniac, that's all."

Shaking her head at me, she laughed. "Jesus, girl. You scared me! Don't do that!"

"Seriously, Mac, don't *you* do that. Don't set me up to be alone with that creep again. I mean it. You might think you're doing the right thing, but trust me, you're not. Nothing good will ever come of Viper and me."

Remembering the almost kiss, I felt a small sliver of disappointment. He'd been all breathy and intense. I wouldn't have stopped him, had he molested me on the busy sidewalk.

Now that my head had cleared though, I was happy it hadn't occurred.

"You know I love you. I just want my friends to be happy. Both you and Viper. I hate seeing the animosity between the two of you and so does Dec."

"Yeah, well, deal with it."

Swigging my cooling coffee, I stood to let her know we were done. Pouring the rest down the sink,

I air kissed her. I couldn't stay too mad no matter how much I wanted to.

Returning it, she called out, "I'll call you."

The day dragged and by six o'clock I couldn't wait to leave. Clocking out, I took the elevator to the basement, finding my SUV where I'd left it in the staff lot.

Shucking my shoes off and throwing them on the passenger seat, I buckled up and drove home, stopping for a bottle of wine on the way. All through my shift, I'd had images of a snarky soldier with an unmovable, ripped body pressing me up to a light pole. His smell. His crazy energy mixed with anger. If Declan was anything like Viper, I could totally understand Mac's obsession. I hated him. I hated the way he spoke to me. Yet among it all, my insides burned to life.

Stepping on the gas after paying for the wine, I made short work of getting home.

I seriously needed to get laid. My preoccupation with a very bad seed proved it. My hormones were in charge and not my head, which, if I wasn't careful, would lead to some disastrous decisions.

Work was chaotic enough. I didn't need my personal life to mimic it.

Walking up the front steps to my condo, juggling my shoes, wine, and handbag, I stooped down and put everything on the concrete porch while I inserted the key into the door. Without warning, a hand covered my mouth from behind. Shocked, I attempted to gasp, but I couldn't. Someone leaned over me, their face close to my ear. The cool feel of metal at my temple stopped my heart momentarily.

My throat dried up and adrenalin made my bloodstream. The sound of it walloped heavily in my ears. Fingers bit into my cheeks as the gun pressed in harder.

"Don't move or attempt to make a sound, bitch, or your head will be splattered all over your porch."

Shit! This couldn't be happening. I didn't know what to do. Unable to speak, I simply nodded as my world slowed. If this nut pulled the trigger, it would all be over in a second. My life. Thoughts sped by in fast motion of never truly living. Is this how Mac had felt during her abduction? I began shaking, hard. I tried to make a sound, but his hand prevented me.

Movement to my left brought another person into my peripheral vision. The only thing I knew was he was dressed in dark attire and reached for my purse.

"Now here's what's going to happen. You're not going to make a scene. If I let you go and you scream, I'll shoot you where you stand. You're going to count to one hundred before you turn around. Understand?"

My head moved up and down on autopilot.

Once my purse disappeared, the ogre behind me thrust my head so hard into the door I saw all the colors of the rainbow before I dropped to the ground. The doormat stopped my knees from ripping open on the concrete.

My breathing consisted of heavy gasps. My head exploded in pain. But I remained conscious, all too aware that if I didn't remain still and as quiet as possible, I'd be feeling a bullet next.

My brain could barely focus on counting so I kneeled, too frightened to do anything else. My purse had been taken, including my cell. I wondered if I'd come straight home instead of stopping for wine, would I have made it inside safely?

I sat shivering for ages until eventually big racking sobs let go and there wasn't a thing I could do to stop them. Had they gone? Were they watching? How long did I stay put?

The bushes rustled beside me, but it could have been the wind which had picked up. I remained frozen, reality hitting home. I'd been robbed. At gunpoint. At freaking gunpoint! I'd never seen a weapon, let alone felt it pushed into my skull. Such a small piece of equipment, yet powerful enough to end me. I listened, silently praying they'd gone. A chill washed over me.

Still, I didn't turn around. I couldn't. Fear held me in its clutches. My hand lifted to my head to feel where it had suffered trauma. Swelling had begun. Groaning, I knew I needed to get inside and lock my door. Looking up, the keys still sat in the door. If the thieves had wanted to, they could have gone inside and taken anything they wanted, but obviously, they needed a quick heist. Probably drug money.

Slowly searching around me, all I found was emptiness.

Pushing up, my skull roared in protest as I shakily found my feet and leaned into the door until the dizziness waned. Not caring if the bottle of wine remained at my feet, I rattled and shook the keys, tears spilling down my cheeks, and then I fell through the door.

My body caved in on itself and I hit the carpet like I weighed a ton. My shoulder jarred as it absorbed the impact and I cried out before rolling over to my back and breaking down completely, the weight of my ordeal suffocating me.

Crying made my whole body ache, but I needed the outlet it provided as I attempted to process the events. It had all happened so fast, giving me no time to react.

My neighborhood had always been safe compared to others, but it became apparent that nobody was safe anywhere.

My apartment echoed with my sobs. The door still hadn't been locked, but I couldn't move. Feeling faint and weak, I closed my eyes. Inside my head it felt like the gun had been fired. I hurt all over.

I couldn't stop myself from fading out completely as pins and needles pricked me like a thousand barbs.

***

Noises stirred me to consciousness. Light seeped into my closed eyes as I attempted to survey my surroundings.

And then an even brighter pinpoint of light was being shone straight at my eyeballs, my eyelids being held open. Blindness took over as the other one had the same procedure.

"Welcome back, Char. You had us all worried."

I knew that voice. My brain just had to play

catchup.

Squinting, needing to see my surroundings, I caught sight of a nurse I recognized.

In a groggy voice, I croaked, "Debbie? What's going on? Why am I here?"

"Honey, you don't remember?"

Closing my eyes again, I let the fog settle. I recalled working yesterday and then returning home. I jolted upright...

"I was hit. Robbed."

Debbie rushed to my bed, gently pushing me back down. "Shhh. It's okay. We're looking after you."

"How? I was at home. How did I get here?" Deep throbbing beat a heavy tempo in my skull, causing me to grimace.

"Do you need some more meds?"

Nodding, I watched her grab two pills from the tray and lift the bed up so I became more vertical. I took the cup and swallowed the pills, hoping they'd hurry the hell up and work.

She still hadn't answered me so I pushed, "How did I get here?"

"Oh." Checking my IV, she smiled. "Mac and two hotties brought you. I recognized one of the said hotties as her John Doe she nursed. The other one, whoa! All male testosterone and fierceness. He had all the nurses want to run for cover and throw their panties at him." A pink blush formed up her neck.

Viper.

"Are they still here?"

I needed to see my friends. I needed Mac.

"Sure. They've been anxiously waiting outside. I'll go get them now that you're awake." She stopped at the door and turned. "You took quite a blow to the head. X-ray showed some minor trauma, but you'll make a full recovery. You'll have quite a headache for a few days. We can have the police come if you'd like to make a statement."

"No!" The last thing I felt like doing was being interrogated. It could wait until tomorrow. I needed to see Mac and Dec first.

Her mouth split into a harsh line but she didn't say anymore as she left.

Still feeling the cool metal pressed to my temple, I shivered. It could have ended tragically. My life could have been snuffed out in a second. Suddenly the pettiness I normally got wound up over didn't seem so important. Being alive and breathing trumped everything.

Watching the door open, emotion washed over me as Mac's worried face appeared, followed by a serious Dec and a pissed off looking Viper.

Mac ran. Her frantic voice became louder. "OMG! Char! What happened? I stopped by for a visit and to apologize after our awkward chat at work. I found your door ajar. When I stepped into your living room and found you unconscious, I thought you were dead!"

She had me in her arms, hugging me. I winced at the sharp pain in my shoulder. The pain meds hadn't kicked in fully yet.

Hearing me, she pushed away. "I'm sorry! Where are you sore?"

"My shoulder from my fall, and my head from

getting bashed into my front door."

"What?" she shrieked. Two burly, protective warriors moved forward, their posture strained.

"Char. Tell me what happened. Who did this to you?" Dec squatted beside the bed, putting us on an even keel while Viper flanked Mac, his arms flexed, muscles bulging. He appeared ready to go into battle. I hoped it wasn't with me, because I couldn't handle his bullshit right now.

Drawing in oxygen in an attempt to replay the event, I turned my head to stare at the ceiling. Mac strode around the bed and grasped my hand in comfort.

"I don't know. I didn't see them."

I hadn't seen faces. I hadn't seen much. Only heard his voice. His deep, caustic voice at my ear.

"Nothing?" Dec pressed, his voice calm, yet I knew he was anything but.

"No. He grabbed me from behind." Feeling anxiety rise and my breathing quicken, I squeezed my eyes tightly shut. "He…he…put a gun to my head."

Mac gasped and squeezed my hand. "Shit. I'm sorry you had to go through that, Char. You don't have to continue. We can come back tomorrow. You just rest."

As my best friend, she could see how shaken I was. Not much rattled me, but now I was teetering on a very fine edge of keeping it together and totally having a meltdown.

Opening my eyes, I looked at the three people surrounding me. Mac had a couple of tears rolling down her face. She pushed some hair from my brow and gently caressed my face. What else could anyone say to that?

Craning my neck to the right, I watched Dec stand and give Viper a worried stare. He turned back to me and said, "Mac's right. You need your rest. You want us to call the cops?"

Viper gripped his friend's shoulder and pulled slightly until they were eyeballing each other again. "Let's check out the place first. See if there's any evidence. I'd like to take a look around before getting the police involved."

Dec nodded. "We'll take care of it, Char, okay? Sleep well, and we'll come visit tomorrow."

"Thank you," I offered, briefly turning my attention to Viper, who hadn't said a word to me. For a second, he radiated pain, but then he turned and walked to the door with Dec on his heels, leaving me with Mac.

"You sure you're gonna be okay?" she asked.

Alone with her, hearing the concern in her voice, I could feel my will crumble. Tears welled.

"I don't know." I sniffled. "I was so scared."

"I know, sweetie."

And if anyone knew, Mac did, which gave me some comfort. She'd endured her own nightmare.

"If they release you tomorrow, I'm not letting you go home alone. I'll worry myself sick."

Suddenly exhausted, just wanting to let go and sleep, I simply replied with, "Whatever."

Kissing my forehead and wiping my tears, which I managed to hold back from flooding out, she whispered. "I'm going to tell the boys to head home. I want to stay a while. Make sure you're okay. I'm just going to authorize it first. I'll be right back."

Thankful that she would stay with me, I sighed. "Thanks, Mac. I really appreciate it.

She left the room and I closed my eyes again. The meds had eased the pain to a dull ache but I was incredibly drowsy. I rolled away to face the window with my back to the door and nodded off.

Chapter Seven

Viper

"Son of a bitch!"

"Easy, man. We'll find the douche. When we do, he's gonna be in a world of pain."

I couldn't focus on the words coming out of Dec's mouth. Rage had me fired up like a bullet about to discharge. I could feel my face and neck burning from the rush of adrenalin. My fists ached from squeezing them so hard.

As much as Red pushed my buttons and drove me insane, the thought of a stranger causing her harm and aiming a pistol at her head had me all kinds of crazy. Seeing her scared and shaken in that hospital bed had me wanting to find the fucker and deface him.

Focusing on my friend as he drove to Charlotte's house, I frowned at his calmness. Normally it was me attempting to restrain him, but for some odd reason, the tables had turned. We'd stopped for some beer, knowing when we got back to my place

I was planning to drown in it.

Slamming my fist onto the dash, once, twice, I ignored the pain, which spread into my wrist. My legs jiggled, just like they did before walking into danger. My blood surged, primed and targeted at my vital organs. I was raring to go, except this time, all the excess testosterone and fire storming my veins had nowhere to go. No outlet. I sat caged in Dec's truck like a freaking wild animal.

"Settle," Dec warned. "I know you, buddy. You're going to be no good to anyone if you don't get a hold of that rage. We need to focus on finding clues. We also need to discuss how best to handle this, whether we call in some favors from our team or go solo."

Turning and lowering my head, I forced my heart to slow by breathing long and hard. Pushing out each breath with my mouth while sucking in deep pulls through my nose. In. Out. In. Out.

"He's dead. Whoever the animal is, I'll kill him with my bare hands."

My self-control teetered. My PTSD warred with my brain. All I could see was the end result. Another waste of space posing as a human taken care of. The world would be a better place.

A memory catapulted me into the nether land of war.

The sounds of the truck's engine dissolved away until rapid gunfire pealed out. Dust and dirt blew us eastward, seeking out enemies, but it seemed our adversaries had found us first.

Diving for cover behind the wreck of a burned

out car, I watched the rest of my team scatter like roaches. Whoever fired first had poor aim because we'd been sitting ducks for the better part of two minutes while scaling down the rocky slope into a small Afghan town. The dwellings had been created from the very mud upon which they sat, branches of trees acting as pillars to assist failing roofs. Swathes of dirty fabric provided door coverings, while most of the windows were simply gaping holes into dark interiors.

The streets, if you could call them that, resembled an off-road trucker's dream with dips and divots haphazardly strewn as far as the eye could see. Whether they were from exploding bombs, or the lack of money and know-how to produce anything better, I wasn't sure. In the millisecond it took to think this, more gunfire sounded. This time closer.

Using my skill and instincts, as soon as the shots ceased, I raised my weapon onto the roof of the charred car and fired off round after round in the direction the enemy sat. So did my team.

Two bodies went down as they'd attempted to close the gap. I needed Dec, but we'd been separated by the initial round of fire. We were all on our own. With instructions to infiltrate and kill, I had no other motive but to fulfill the request to the letter while not getting myself taken down in the process. This is what fed my soul. This moment. The quiet, unknowing when not even a breeze stirred. I licked my parched lips, needing fluid but knowing I needed to push the thirst to the back of the queue of things to do. Seek and destroy first. Eat and drink later.

Feeling a bullet suddenly whizz past me, I hit the dirt, spinning around for the source. My veins throbbed with the rush of blood. My finger itched on the trigger as I sighted up, ready. Scoping the area, I looked to where I thought Dec might be. With my hawk-like vision, as I faced the dilapidated shack closest to me, I garnered movement at the back of the building. Swinging my weapon around, sharp and focused, I breathed out when I watched Dec emerge, pointing inside the building. That must have been where the close shot came from. We needed to get in and end it.

Clearing the way for me, four heavily armed soldiers followed Dec, firing random shots around the expanse so my commanding officer and I could proceed.

Sprinting across the space to meet my friend, he pushed me behind him, letting me know he was in charge and leading the mission. I also knew that it went beyond the duty of his rank. He wanted to protect me like a brother.

Turning to me and holding up four fingers in our traditional countdown, he let his fingers fall one by one so that when the last one folded down, we moved. Quickly and precisely, our guys still fired off shots.

Inching along the wall toward a window, we both ducked low and crawled underneath so as not to be seen. Dec motioned to the troops to cease fire but remain vigilant. It was sign language we all knew well.

Not waiting for another countdown but acting on

a single nod, I followed Dec into the slum. It was sparse with a table and two chairs which had been overturned and a few personal items scattered around. A dirty chair sat in one corner with an even dirtier rug in front of it.

Something hit me on my upper arm and stung like a bitch. Burning momentarily made me lose focus to process that I'd been shot. Dec didn't falter as I gritted my teeth and began firing. He was on the move, so I followed through the squalor to the only other room we could see. A movement as we neared had me forget about my bleeding wound. Kill. Maim. Destroy. A mantra swallowed any other thoughts.

We hadn't spoken a word and still moved like ghosts. More shots fired, halting our entry further. Plastered against the wall, Dec quickly glanced at me and I put my thumb up to let him know I was okay.

I'd suffered worse. Much worse.

Nodding to give me approval, I swung only the barrel of my weapon into the room and fired.

Dec did the same.

Grunts and wails followed by thuds let us know we'd hit our targets, so we risked it all and moved through the opening.

Three more bodies lay on the ground. Two still. One moving and attempting to reload his weapon. Too late, sunshine. Time to play.

Still aiming at his chest, I lowered my weapon to the hand attempting to fumble for his gun. Blood oozed from his thigh and more seeped out of his shoulder. We could just let him bleed out but where would the fun in that be?

This animal didn't deserve the air he breathed. He killed for fun and now it was my turn to give him a taste of his own medicine. Scum.

Grinning at him, I pulled the trigger, blowing a hole in his hand. He screamed, thrusting his head back in pain as I neared. Dec searched the dwelling, letting me party. The douche had a mark on him for death anyway.

He dragged his head back down to look at me, hatred and agony evident. I didn't blink. I had no compassion toward the enemy. His bloodied stump rested up across his chest, his other hand clutching just above it as if that might help ease the pain.

Dec finished his thorough search and returned to my side. "Finish it. We need to move," he ordered.

Further adrenalin drove me into a pre-kill frenzy. Bending down, I gripped my prey's arm and pulled it down to the floor, holding it there while I placed my boot heavily down on the macabre remains of a hand that had killed and maimed innocent villagers.

Hearing the wretched moans and his weak attempt at trying to pull his arm away, I laughed, lining up my barrel to his leg where I knew the femoral artery ran. This dude deserved a slow and painful death.

Firing one round, I rose, saluting the dreg of society before following Dec outside.

"You okay, man?" he asked.

Why would he ask me that? He knew me better than to ask if I was okay.

I stared at him.

"Viper! Viper! You with me?"

Spiraling back into the present, I found two hands shaking me, a worried frown cutting into Dec's brow.

Shaking off my reverie, I nodded, pushing him away.

"Jesus. Where were you?" he asked, leaning back into his own seat. We'd stopped driving and had parked outside Char's apartment.

Fisting both of my eyes to clear my head, I opened the truck door. "Taking out the trash."

Slamming the door, I strode purposefully toward the door of Red's home, intent on looking for clues to help rid society of more insects.

The crime had happened outside, so if evidence remained, we wouldn't need to enter.

"Hey!" A hand on my arm. Pulling me around.

Dec's face held grave concern.

"What's going on? You look like you're about to go on a killing spree. Something's changed with you. Normally you're cool and collected. I've noticed lately you're battling some sort of inner demon. You not coping anymore?"

He didn't need to clarify. He asked if I was losing my grip on my PTSD. He knew me too well.

Raking a hand over the top of my head, I sighed. "I don't know, man. Ever since I had to save your ass, I've been experiencing things."

"Things?" He let me go and stood firm directly in front of me, like the commanding officer he was.

Letting words drip from my mouth unfiltered, I rambled, "I think I like killing. I feel like I can't survive without it, and yet another part of me feels like a monster." Turning away from him, I stepped forward, stopping and gripping my head. "I have so many visions popping into my head of our time at war. I really am a sick bastard. How can anyone enjoy taking another's life, regardless of what they've done?"

Shame threatened to bring me to my knees. I couldn't look at Dec. A small sliver of relief held me in its grip at my confession, but it was minor compared to the war raging within.

I could feel when he stopped behind me.

"Talk to me."

Swallowing hard, I still couldn't eye him. "You ever miss the thrill of battle? The adrenalin?"

"Of course! We're soldiers. It's what we do. We love our jobs or we wouldn't be doing it."

My head shot to his, not expecting to hear him sound so enthusiastic after all he'd endured.

"You still love it?" I asked, shocked.

"Yep. That's not to say I exactly like taking a life, but it's us or them. We're the good guys. We don't go around beheading and aimlessly killing innocents. We serve to protect."

Sighing out a huge breath, I continued, needing him to understand. "Maybe, but my dreams are all about the killing part. Not about the saving innocent lives. What does that even mean?"

"You taking your meds?"

Scratching my face, I answered, "Yeah. I'm on the strongest dose."

Watching headlights brighten, waiting for a vehicle to drive past us, I anticipated my friend's advice. I needed him to tell me I wasn't going crazy. Special Ops soldiers had to be tough. Our minds had to be like machines. Closed off and untouchable to the aftereffects of war. Special types of people who could disassociate themselves from it all. I'd been that warrior. I'd never batted an eyelid in the most horrific of situations for a good part of my career. But what if the human brain could only take so much? What if our inner computers weren't hardwired to retain so much horror? What if eventually, it changed us? Fucked us up. Were human beings, even cold, hardened ones, meant to witness such evil and not have it alter them in some way?

Another what if. What if all the killing I'd done had turned me into a psychopath?

"Okay. Answer me this." His deep voice pulled me from my own head. "Have you ever had the desire to kill an innocent man?"

"No!"

"Woman?"

"No!"

"Child?"

"Of course not! Never."

"Right then. So you're not a monster. You only take care of the ones we're ordered to destroy. You do your job and you're fucking brilliant at it. I wouldn't be here if it weren't for you, and neither would Mac. You care about those close to you. You'd lay down your own life for them. That's not something a crazy person would do. Don't you see? You're not getting off on killing the scum of the earth, you're getting off on ridding the world of evil. You're relieved they can't hurt anyone else. By terminating the bad seeds, you're potentially saving hundreds more."

His eyes drilled into me like his words. Could he be right? Could there be some goodness left in me?

Char's words flooded my brain. She's told me I looked like I wanted to hit her and to 'just do it.' My immediate reaction had been one of repulsion. I had never nor would never hit a woman and I had no inclination to do so. The same with children. Men? Only if they threatened me or those close to me.

Dec gripped both my shoulders and shook me. "Hey! You hear where I'm coming from? You're a good person. War affects all of us, no matter how tough we are. We're still human, after all." Watching me nod, he asked, "You gonna be okay? You ready to search for clues now?"

"Yeah. Thanks, man. Let's do it."

Chapter Eight

Char

The next morning, I awoke to a familiar nurse taking my temperature and changing my IV bag. Gaining my bearings, remembering I was in the hospital, I searched for Mac, finding her asleep on a chair in the corner. She'd stayed all night? Bless her! But she didn't look comfortable, scrunched up on the hard chair.

"How are you feeling this morning, Char?" Debbie had been replaced by Martine, a middle-aged woman with four grown children. Her husband had passed from cancer twelve months ago, so working at the hospital had proved to be her life-line. She smiled cheerily at me.

"Like I've been in a boxing ring," I groaned out.

My voice woke Mac. She squinted, rubbing her eyes before standing and stretching, then walking over to me.

"Hey, girl. You look better than you did last night."

"Liar." I huffed, sure that she was just saying it to appease me.

Leaning down, she kissed my cheek. "You may not feel it, but you look more lucid."

Martine fluffed my pillows and checked my pulse, adding to the conversation. "What's it like being the patient in this place? Is the service any good?" She winked and grinned, attempting a joke.

Actually, everyone had been super nice. It made me proud to be part of such a great team.

"It's a pain being laid up even for a few hours, but the level of care is second to none. You guys are amazing."

"It takes one to know one, girl. You're just as amazing. I'm sure you'll be getting home today after a scan. A little birdie told me you're getting a week off, paid."

Not wanting to be idle for too long and worried about returning to my apartment, I looked to Mac. "We'll see. I'll probably return sooner than that."

Shaking her head with a firm set to her mouth, Mac disputed my claim. "Ah, no, you won't be. I'll tie you down if I have to. You're taking some time off and will not argue about it."

She could be a tough nut if she wanted to. I knew by her tone that I'd be silly to argue with her. I wasn't in the mood to resist anyone.

"Fine, but I don't want to return to my apartment."

With Mac and Dec together every night at either one of their homes, I wasn't sure where I'd go.

Martine finished up. "I'd love to stay and chat, ladies, but I have rounds to do. You get better and stay out of trouble, you hear me?" She tried to give me a stern warning, but I knew it was out of love and concern.

"Thanks, Martine. I'll try."

Giving her my best smile, she happily wandered off.

Mac glanced at me, down to the floor, and then back, biting the inside of her mouth. "Sooo, I know you probably don't like what I'm about to say, but I think you should move in with Viper for now. Until the perp is caught."

Widening my eyes at her absurd suggestion, I balked. "Are you freaking kidding me? What happened to you butting out of trying to put me within hitting distance of that…that…frustrating man!"

Chuckling, she added, "Before you go off on a rant, think about it. I would have you stay with me, but then you'll feel like a third wheel." Blushing, she continued, "Plus, ah, Dec isn't always quiet…"

"Duh. I have heard his voice. He's got that deep rumble going on."

"I'm not talking about during the day." Waiting, she stared at me a moment before my brows lifted in understanding.

"Oh. Gotcha. Ahem, well then. Yeah, that might be kind of embarrassing. For you, I mean."

Mac laughed, fully. Could I handle hearing them go at it like rabbits? Ugh. Probably not.

That left me in a quandary.

"You can't rein in your vocal pleasure for me?"

Perching on the edge of my bed, she patted my hand. "I can, but Dec, I'm not so sure. When he releases…it's like…"

Before she could give me all the sordid details, I stopped her. "Don't! Normally I'd love hearing all the dirty details, but I'm not feeling it today. I want out of here, but I don't want to go home."

Mac's face grimaced as she mulled over my dilemma. "You know what? Screw Dec. Excuse the pun, but you're my best friend. You come first. He can either quiet the hell down during sex or move in with Viper!" Leaning over me in a quick hug, she said, "I'm so sorry for not putting you first."

And then my own guilt hit. Did I really expect my friend to give up the one thing she'd finally found? She was happy in spite of her own recent drama. She'd had enough to deal with and she and Dec were helping each other overcome all their hurdles. I couldn't be selfish and expect her to take me in and give up her happiness to babysit me because I was too chicken to face my apartment and be alone.

No. I wouldn't do that to her. I needed to do the one thing I knew I'd regret.

"Actually, don't apologize. I'm the one who should be doing that to you." Through gritted teeth and with muscles in my neck wound so tightly they caused pain, I stuttered, "I'll move in with Viper, only until I can stand to be on my own."

Her expression became one of concerned horror. "But what about before? You balking at me even suggesting the idea?"

Sinking back into the pillow, I glanced away. "I don't like it. I don't. But I also don't want you kicking Dec out because of me. You've only just found your Prince Charming. I mean it. I'll be fine. After a week I'll be working again, and I'll only have to see him at night. It won't be that bad, right?"

If she saw through my lie, she didn't say anything. A grin formed on her face and her eyes twinkled. "I'll come visit often too, I promise. Viper will protect you, don't worry. You'll be safe with him."

I might be safe physically, but mentally could be a whole other story.

"Does Viper even know of your absurd plan?"

"I kind of ran it by him and Dec before coming here."

Of course she did. She had it all figured out. "And? I bet he wasn't too happy."

Reaching for the glass of water off the side table, she handed it to me without thinking. Her nurse instincts were never far from the surface. Taking the glass, I sipped, enjoying the liquid on my dry lips. '

"Let's just say, he agreed."

Right. After much arguing. I'd bet a week's wages on it.

"I don't know about this, Mac. I hardly know the guy."

"You'll be fine. He's sweet when you get to know him."

That may all be well and good, but the guy hated me, and while hate was a very strong word, he wasn't high on my friend's list. What had I done?

"Give it a few days. If you still decide you don't want to be there, I'll pick you up and take you to my place like I suggested."

Taking a deep grounding breath, I nodded, happy to have an out if I needed one.

I placed the glass back. "Thanks for staying the night, Mac. You really should have gone home. That chair over there does not look comfortable."

"And leave you scared and vulnerable? I couldn't do that to you. I'm here for you, no matter what."

I knew she meant it. She'd proved it many times. I was so grateful to have her in my life.

"Thank you. It means a lot."

***

After Mac left to go to my apartment and pack some things for me, I had my scan and got the all clear to leave, thankfully. Mac returned with my overnight bag and keys. With pain meds in hand, we made our way to Mac's Mustang. My head still pounded, but it was to be expected after the blow I took. I felt naked without my purse and cell. I'd need to cancel my credit cards. The assholes who assaulted me had probably already run up a huge bill. Plus, I'd need to get a new phone. Luckily it was always kept locked, so the thugs couldn't access anything.

Nerves stirred in my belly at the notion of seeing Viper again, let alone living with him short-term. We'd tear each other's heads off. In which case, I'd be moving in with Mac and Dec and ignoring whatever sounds came from their bedroom. I could do that, right? Ugh. Couldn't they just abstain while I was there? I knew Dec had a high sex drive from my friend's colorful descriptions, but I mean, come on.

"You okay?" Mac asked, stealing my vision.

Pulling in to a modestly kept suburban home, shivers dotted my arms and legs. My gut roiled further. Handing the driver the twenty Mac had left for me, I exited.

Before my door had shut, the automatic garage door began rising, revealing Viper's truck.

My heart ratcheted up a notch, and suddenly I felt as if it was my first day in foster care.

The next thing I spotted was a pair of bare feet, denim-clad legs, followed by the overwhelming sight of a bare torso, twisting as Viper threw on a tee. Damn. I didn't want to look or like his worked abs of corrugated iron. Or the black tattoo which almost resembled a tribal emblem that drove upward from his groin to someplace north.

His heavy strides broke my haze as he thundered forward to embrace Mac fully. "Hey you, yourself! Good to see you. How's the douchebag?"

Perhaps I wasn't the only one he was a dick to. Perhaps that was just his normal way with people. He sure seemed to like calling his best friend names.

On guard, I watched silently as they greeted each other before Mac turned to me and then back to Viper. He hadn't given me an ounce of his time so far but finally acknowledged my presence.

"Red."

That was it?

Already my blood heated. Turning on my heels, I pulled open the driver's door of the Mustang and released the trunk lever, slamming the door and moving to grab my bags.

Attempting to drag it out, I struggled, wondering what Mac had put in it.

A second later, I was knocked aside as large arms came into focus beside me, easily lifting the suitcase out as if it weighed no more than an ounce.

"I could have grabbed it." I huffed, steadying myself again.

"You've just come from the hospital. I got it." Closing the trunk, he began walking inside, leaving Mac and me with no option but to follow.

The interior of his house surprised me. I didn't know what I'd expected, but neatness and order hadn't been it for a male living on his own. Then again, he was a soldier, so I guess he'd had it drummed into him since joining the military. Impressed, I moved further into the living room, not sure what to do next.

Viper strolled down the hallway with my case, calling out, "You coming to see where your room is?"

Siding a peek at Mac, I could have punched the smile off her face. Smugness didn't become her. Huffing as I walked past her, I followed Viper's voice down the end of the hallway to a small room on the right.

With a double bed sitting against the middle of the right wall, the space lessened considerably. A timber wardrobe sat just inside the door to the left with clothing drawers opposite the bed. Apart from that, the beige colored room held no feeling of comfort. Reminding myself I would only be occupying it a short time, I held my place in the doorway with Mac at my heels.

Viper placed my suitcase on the edge of the bed. He appeared as unsettled as I was.

Seeking my gaze before settling on the carpet he mumbled, "Towels are in the hall cupboard. Bathroom is the first door on the right."

It was the nicest thing I had heard from him, even if it had felt forced.

"Thanks," I grumbled back, moving aside to let him out the door when he began moving toward me.

"Okay. That's settled then. Will you be okay, Char? Is there anything you need before I leave?"

A knot formed in my throat, disabling my ability to speak, so I simply shook my head.

When she padded away, I moved with her, wishing she could stay a while longer.

Fatigue had me needing a nap, but first I had to take some more meds to help ease the vise squeezing my head.

When I found the kitchen, I began searching the cupboards for a glass. I heard Mac speaking quietly to Viper before she came in and hugged me.

In a quiet voice, she said, "Call me if you need me."

"Okay." Squeezing her for a moment too long, I let her go and swigged some water with three pills, hoping they'd knock me out for a week so I could leave and go to Mac's.

When the click of the front door sounded, the quietness settled in. A hulk of a body appeared, seemingly out of his depth.

"Um, do you need anything? Are you hungry?"

Was I? Considering every time 'said' male came within three feet of me, causing my insides to knot up, I'd say no. But I'd only eaten the hospital breakfast and knew I needed to keep my strength up. That's what I'd have told any of my patients on returning home after an injury.

"Yeah, actually, that would be nice."

Were we actually having a conversation without tearing into each other? I'd never have thought it possible. Maybe he was trying now that he had no choice.

Easing around the kitchen fluidly, I watched as he opened the freezer and pulled out some chicken, and then squatted to the chiller section in the bottom of the fridge and loaded up his arms with fresh vegetables.

Wow. Impressive. A man who knew his way around a kitchen and who appeared to be able to cook.

"Chicken stir-fry okay?" His arms bulged as he placed the veggies down on the bench beside the cutting board.

"Sounds good. I...uh...didn't know you could cook."

"There's a lot you don't know about me, Red. I've been on my own a while. It's a case of having to. Wine?"

Catching me off guard by his sudden politeness, I stammered, "Y...yes." Who was this man? Had I judged him too soon?

His eyes lifted to mine at my faltering, but he remained silent, lifting a bottle of red wine from the fridge while getting two glasses out of another cupboard with one hand. Placing mine down on the counter, he ordered, "Sit."

His head nodded to the chair at the small wooden kitchen table, so I complied, still in a daze, and surprised that I felt mildly comfortable.

Knowing wine and pain meds weren't a good combination, but needing something to distract me from the multi-faceted male pouring my drink, I took a large swig when he'd finished, loving the taste.

Viper sipped at his own drink while he set about preparing an early dinner. My watch read four thirty p.m. Early for me, considering I normally didn't eat until around seven thirty, depending on when I got home from work.

Viper turned from the stove as I tried to cover a big yawn. "Am I keeping you up?"

He could keep me up anytime, my damn brain silently said to me.

"I won't lie. I'm beat. I'll probably just eat, shower, and go to bed."

"Whatever you need to get better."

Spinning back to the pan, my eyes traced the curve of his shoulders and back, down further to his molded ass. He filled out a pair of jeans like a man should. The denim clung to his cheeks perfectly, and by God, I almost choked on a swallow. The proportions of the man had been crafted by the Chief Upstairs himself, without a doubt. My naughty mind, spurred on by another giant swig of wine and the painkillers, had me imagining that ass above me, all clenched and sweaty.

"Staring is rude, you know!" came his bark,

causing me to jump. He still hadn't turned around, so I decided to act dumb.

"What? I'm not even looking your way."

"Uh huh! Lie all you want. I could feel your eyes burning a hole in my back."

Holy shit! Was he psychic too? Psycho, definitely.

The arm holding the wooden stirring spoon flexed as he gripped the handle tightly.

The air thickened and I suddenly needed to escape.

"I'm just gonna go take that shower. Leave my dinner on the table."

Getting up and practically running down the hallway to my room, I pulled a tank and some sleep shorts from my bag and quickly locked myself in the bathroom, breathing way too heavily for someone who hated the male in the kitchen.

Stripping, I stared at my reflection, the woman peering back changed. I'd never be the same again after having a gun at my head. The realization of how quickly everything could be taken away at the hands of strangers made tears well. I felt wrung out. On a giant sob, I stripped and stepped into the shower, turning on the faucets and feeling the sting of the cold water stab at my skin like daggers, but not caring because the pain inside cut me worse.

A wail left me as my back slid down the tiles until I sat on the shower floor, knees bent. The warmth from the hot tap came through, but it may as well have remained cold because all I could feel was the barrel of a gun, probably loaded, ready to blow my brains out. One flinch or itchy finger could have ended it all for me. I'd now be lying in a morgue.

Closing my eyes, I sobbed, feeling detached and alien. Where had I gone? I suddenly didn't resemble Char anymore. She'd been carefree and relatively happy. This new version had lost something during the robbery. I couldn't pinpoint what that *something* was though. I just knew it was missing. Trust? Peace? Ignorance? Perhaps all three.

I knew I could talk to Mac, but here in Viper's bathroom, enclosed within the four walls, an incredible sense of loneliness gripped me.

It tore me open from the inside out like a giant crevasse. Moments ago I'd been sitting ogling an arrogant, confusing, yet hot male, and now I couldn't even pick myself up from the bottom of the shower stall. Despair and hopelessness carried me away. I sunk into the nightmare playing over and over in my mind. Tormenting me. Attempting to break my will.

I let go completely, shaking and inconsolable.

I didn't feel my body being lifted because when I came to I was moving, crushed up against steel coated in velvet. My face pressed against skin, a tempo beating underneath it.

Blinking and focusing more, I realized vaguely Viper must have broken the bathroom door down and picked me up. Carefully I was placed down on a soft bed. Deep murmurings echoed closely as I felt the bed dip beside me.

Blanketed by warmth akin to a furnace, I settled, letting it seep into my pores. A strong arm came under me and pulled me in closer.

"I got you. Sleep now, Red."
Darkness washed over me.

***

Disoriented and stiff, I attempted to roll over, but I had been pinned down on my back. Opening my eyes, a heaviness draped over me. My skin burned and beads of sweat slithered down my brow.

Realizing Viper had attached himself to me like jellyfish tentacles, my breath caught. Every part of him was pressed into and across me. Only half of my body remained visible. He'd kept his jeans on, but his upper body was naked. Oh, my! His head was pressed into my neck so that his deep breathing blew wisps of hot air onto my skin. One leg crossed over both of mine, and his torso, which weighed a ton, had my right breast mashed underneath.

I desperately needed to pee but didn't know how to go about waking him. I was pretty sure when he realized how close we were he would go all psycho again, and to be honest, I'd enjoyed his more placid side before I'd had my meltdown.

Holding off for a moment, I simply basked in the feel of him. It had been way too long since I'd woken in bed with a man. And never had I awoken with a soldier whose muscles were chiseled to perfection. I could still smell remnants of shampoo in his hair and flickers of aftershave accented the aroma. Hell. I was in fiery, sizzling glorious hell.

My bladder threatened to explode, so I had no choice but to move. Pushing out from under him, he stirred and I froze, wondering what his reaction would be.

"Hmmm," he mumbled, rolling onto his back and flinging an arm over his face. Light had begun seeping in at the corners of the closed blinds. Checking him out some more, I gasped at the bulge in his groin. Crap! Had I done that? Or was it simply a case of male morning wood?

Inching off the bed, I furtively kept watch. Just as I thought I was home free with just my knee on the mattress, arresting hazel eyes pinned me in place.

I felt mortified. Like I'd done something wrong. His bleary eyes blinked a couple of times and then cleared. The moment recognition set in, he sat up ramrod straight. He scanned me from head to knee, where I still perched like I'd turned to stone. He paused at my bare legs and then found my chest, which I was afraid to look at because the tingling washing over me led me to believe my nipples had betrayed me and hardened.

His jaw tightened. "Uh, I need to go. You okay to get breakfast? There's food in the cupboard." He turned from me, rose, and walked into the bathroom connected to his room without a glance back.

I whispered a "yes," which I doubt he even heard as the door slammed shut.

Just as I'd suspected, except without a verbal lashing.

It wasn't my fault. He could have left me in the shower. He hadn't needed to carry me to bed, strip his shirt off, and crawl in beside me.

I got you. I got you. I got you. The words rang in my head like some damn melody. Why had he said those words last night and this morning he couldn't escape me quick enough? Gah! Frustrating didn't cover the man. Then again, wouldn't anyone have said the same words to another person on the verge of a breakdown?

The shower switched on, so I headed to the second bathroom to pee before moving to the kitchen to make coffee and breakfast, not knowing what I was supposed to do all day. Not one to sit idly, I checked the freezer and found some bacon, then found the eggs sitting in a bowl on a counter beside the cooktop.

Searching the cupboards, I grabbed a pan and set about making breakfast, needing to keep busy or my mind would unravel back to my ordeal. Waking next to Viper had helped push things aside temporarily, but I wasn't sure how long that would last without me succumbing to a panic attack or worse.

Mac would be working all day, so there wasn't really anyone I could call on. My parents lived in Dallas, along with most of my cousins, and my two brothers were scattered. One lived in London, working for a law firm, and the other was traveling around Europe like a wandering nomad. Half his luck. The idea of it sounded pretty good. Taking off wherever and whenever I felt like it. Being that free.

I'd been posted in Ann Arbor for my internship and had stayed on at University Hospital ever since. The town had grown on me and I'd met Mac and settled into a comfortable life. Nothing had ever really bothered me. Until my attack. Now I wondered if I could remain in the town that has given me everything and then taken it just as quickly.

Flipping the eggs and bacon, I lowered the heat and set the table for two. Viper would be hungry, and I didn't want to seem like I was mooching off him while I was here. I'd earn my keep.

Actually, the idea of cooking for someone else made me smile. It seemed homely and normal. Often, before work, I'd grab a protein bar or something and be on my way. A fully cooked breakfast was a rarity.

Hearing a sound behind me, I spun to find Viper standing in the kitchen opening, hand in his hair, an odd look on his face as he watched me dish up the food. He had paused and so had I. If I'd thought he looked edible when I'd woken earlier, he had just fully surpassed that.

Wet scalp with his short haircut spiky all over with droplets easing a slow path down the side of his face and neck, which he made no move to wipe away. His low hanging sweats told me there was a trail of mass destruction slightly further south. His pecs mounded above his eight pack that resembled corrugated iron, and I officially was a goner. Swooning when I had no business doing so because I hated the guy. Remember? Hated with a passion. Even the word passion had me blush as I thought it.

I raised my head and found him glancing between the table and me as if my making him breakfast confused him.

"Ahh, I hope you don't mind. I was kind of hungry."

Since when did I sound like such a timid mouse?

Confident Char had left the building with Elvis. The view in front of me made me nervous to the point of not being able to form an adult sentence.

His slight nod pleased me because he hadn't gone all rogue and asked what the hell I thought I was doing. He did speak, though. "You gonna dish that last piece of bacon up or stand there gawking all day?"

Spell officially broken. Looking down, I noticed the tongs were dangling above his plate with the bacon scrunched up.

Dropping it onto his plate, I turned and put the pan in the sink, sucking in a breath as if it might be my last, the air suddenly very thin.

Chill, Char. You can do this. You can sit and eat a civil meal without an argument or saying anything snide. He has taken you into his home, so be nice no matter what. Be the bigger person.

The chair scraped out as he sat, my back still facing him. Steeling myself for the sight I'd have to get used to, I managed to mask my interest in his body and shuffle to the chair opposite.

My plate became my focus as I shoveled the bacon in, not caring if I resembled a pig. The hollow empty feeling inside needed filling and bacon had jumped to the top of the list.

Viper cleared his throat. "Umm, about this morning. I…uh…was asleep and didn't know what I was doing."

Keep your eyes on your food, Char. Don't look. Don't look. So he had known I'd been cocooned underneath him for a good portion of the night. And now the excuses came. Of course.

"Whatever. It meant nothing." Liar. Needing to swallow my pride, I continued, talking to my cooling eggs. "Thank you."

A long breath out sounded and then the clang of a fork being placed down. "For?"

Oh, don't give me that. Don't make me spell it out for you.

"For, you know. Getting me out of the shower. I don't remember you breaking the door down."

More heavy breathing. I couldn't keep my head down any longer. Slowly and painfully I raised my chin, taking him in from the waist up as I went. Dear Mother of God. He better not think he could walk around shirtless the whole time I stayed because that would be just plain cruel.

"I'm not in the habit of saving damsels in distress, but you sounded…broken." He frowned, his mouth flattening. Eyes wounded.

Embarrassed he'd witness that, I whispered, "I'm sorry."

Slanting his head slightly as if garnering my mood, he offered, "Don't apologize, Red. Happens to all of us."

Realizing he'd been through way more than me, and suddenly feeling like a wuss, I asked, "How do you do it? Cope, I mean."

"Deal?" He laughed but it wasn't filled with humor. More like sarcasm. "You think I deal with everything?"

"I guess. You always seem so…cool and in control."

He licked some of the bacon fat off his lips, leaving them glistening. I rose and poured myself a glass of water, needing to cool the burn. Swigging the entire glass, I filled it again before returning to my place.

"Like I've said before, you don't know me." It came out angry.

"You're right, I don't, but hopefully we can get to know each other a little more while I'm here."

He glared at me, nostrils flaring. Without another word and food still on his plate, he thrust his chair back, picked up a set of keys from the counter, and strode out through the door into the garage. When his SUV tore away, I wondered again what the hell I'd said or done. Talk about moody females. They had nothing on Viper.

My appetite suddenly waned, leaving me with a churned stomach. What an ass. I'd been attempting civility between us and thought we'd been making progress but obviously not.

At this rate, I'd be calling Mac and telling her I wanted to leave today.

Chapter Nine

Viper

Damn woman! My house walls were closing in around me with her there. I should never have agreed to let her stay. Those fucking wounded green eyes got me every time and I hated it.

Finding her in my shower, unable to form coherent words last night had chipped away a layer of my shield. Carrying her crumpled body into my bed, like some wounded soldier I'd had to pull out of harm's way, my inner rescue warrior had taken over. Get to safety at all costs. But it had been more than instinct. Feeling her soft, wet skin beneath my fingers, her tangled red mane hanging loosely after I'd returned to the bathroom for a towel to dry it, had nudged a faraway place inside of me I wanted to keep locked in the vault. Opening the doors to my vulnerable side only caused pain. Weakness. If there was one thing I'd had driven into me years earlier was in order to cut it as one of the military elite, weakness wasn't tolerated. Weakness was reserved for pussies who weren't protecting their countries.

Why then, seeing Char in such a vulnerable state, had I felt the need to comfort her? Viper the badass didn't do comfort. Especially not to a frustrating woman whose fire only served to fuel mine. It didn't make sense. So when she'd gone all sappy about wanting to get along and know me better, I'd stormed out.

The very real fact that I'd somehow unconsciously draped myself around her in the night, feeling her glorious body soft under my steel, had me all kinds of jittery. The hard on that had come with it couldn't be explained any other way except she was stunning. Under normal circumstances and if I were a normal civilian, she would have been screaming my name real quick. But I wasn't normal. Couldn't ever be normal.

I'd become a prisoner of war in my own head. Shackled to the thrill of fighting. The necessity to be part of a finely tuned team. Invisible iron bars caging me into all things war.

Pulling into the lot of Forest Hill Cemetery, I killed the engine and sat in a stupor, wondering how I'd managed to steer my way across town without crashing.

A wind had picked up, thrusting dry leaves across the hood of my vehicle. Trees rustled as I opened my door and walked the familiar route.

Most people disliked graveyards, but I found an odd comfort in them. Perhaps because I knew my parents rested in the fourth row down and I found refuge in the quiet solitude of such hallowed ground.

Stopping in front of a double headstone, I bowed my head, saying a prayer before sitting on the raised concrete burial plot.

"Hey, Mom. Dad. It's been a while since I last visited. Things have been kind of crazy. But you knew my life was never going to be normal when I enlisted."

Sighing, I glanced around the cemetery. I had the place to myself. Fresh flowers adorned some headstones while others decayed, the writing barely visible.

"I miss you guys. Dad, even though you were tough on me, I see now you were only trying to teach me right from wrong. It helped me become the soldier I am today. It taught me to be able to stand on my own two feet. To be independent and not needy. I couldn't see it at the time and thought you were just being a dick, but I see now. Everything you pushed at me, everything you corrected me on, hardened me for battle. I wouldn't have survived the military otherwise. Mom. Dear, sweet Mom. How I miss your hugs. Your faith in me. I can't imagine what you went through when I went to war. The stress you must have endured. You never once asked me to give up what I loved even though it killed you inside, not knowing whether your only son would return. You tried to keep the good in me. But I feel like I failed you. I'm not good. Not anymore. War forced it out of me. My very passion destroyed the one thing you wanted to remain within me. Now I don't know who I am. Who I've become."

A car pulled up a little way away. Turning, I watched an elderly man and woman get out and walk to a grave, flowers in hand. Kneeling, they placed the fresh bouquets down in place of the ones which had withered and died. Sadness surrounded them. Son? Daughter? Who knew? Like me, they had lost a part of themselves and only had this place to feel closer to their loved ones.

Rising, I felt calmer than when I'd stormed out of the house. Guilt swamped me at leaving Char vulnerable. My folks would be horrified at the way I'd treated her. My dad would have kicked my butt. One thing he'd always instilled in me was to respect others. That same respect had been shot out of me. Starved from my system when I'd had no food for days. Smashed to smithereens along with the ten bones I'd broken in my body during battle. I barely had respect for myself, let alone anyone else. The only person I could say I truly and utterly respected was Dec. He deserved every ounce of my veneration.

"I'll be back soon. I love and miss you both more than you'll ever know."

Walking to my vehicle, for the first time in a long while my eyes twitched with unshed tears. Tears that should have fallen but couldn't. I wouldn't allow them to. I couldn't. If the dam broke, I'd drown.

At a loose end, not knowing what to do but unable to return home, I drove.

***

Hours later after stopping for a bite to eat at Grand Haven, needing fresh air and sunshine, I returned home.

The house was quiet when I entered from the garage into the kitchen. Checking the living room, I found it vacant as well.

Stepping into the hallway, a sound broke through. My keen sense of hearing knew it came from Char's room. Quietly stepping forward, I stopped outside the door, which sat ajar only enough for me to confirm the sound. Crying.

Shit! What did I do with that? Now that I knew she was upset, I couldn't just walk away like I hadn't heard it. She must have known I had returned. The garage door wasn't exactly quiet.

Or was she so distressed, she hadn't heard a thing?

Pushing the door open, my insides fissured. Lying on the bed, curled up into the fetal position, hair a tangled mess, cheeks stained with tears, lay Char. She didn't register my appearance as I stalked closer. Had she been crying all day? It looked like she had. Damn. Had I been selfish in leaving her? I only had myself to think about normally.

"Red?" I asked, voice strangely sincere.

She sniffed but didn't lift her head.

Moving to the edge of the bed and sitting, my hand itched to reach out to pull the streaked hair from her face. Even in her current state, she would leave most women for dead in the looks department.

My fingers itched. Throat dry, I scratched out, "Did something happen while I was out?"

Of course something happened. Look at her,

dude. Such a dumb ass question.

"Can I get you anything?"

Finally, her head lifted as if it weighed a ton. Her splintered green eyes met mine, causing my heart to stutter. The strong, feisty redhead had been replaced by someone I didn't recognize. Vulnerability surrounded her. Sadness seeped from her pores, and all I wanted to do was search for the fuckers that had made her like this and tear their heads from their shoulders.

Her lips quivered as she managed to get out four words that robbed me of any thoughts other than, *comfort her.* Four words. Each syllable was drawn out. "I. Feel. Dead. Inside."

That was it. I reached for her, unable to watch her crumble any more. I knew that feeling all too well. I'd experienced it numerous times and I wouldn't wish it on anyone. Least of all a woman.

For the second time in as many days, my soldier receded, allowing a portion of myself I barely recognized to come forth. Some instinctive part that hadn't been created or destroyed by war. It lived under all the muck.

She clung on as if I were her only lifeline, and perhaps I was right now. I rubbed circles on her back and lowered my head to her hair, brushing my cheek over her soft strands. Small hands gripped my shirt as I pulled her up and onto my lap like a small child.

"Let it out, Red. I'll catch you."

Sobbing loudly, her tears wet my shirt. I held her as if she might break further. My large form swallowed her up as I wrapped her around me.

I found myself rocking like I was the one needing comfort. Perhaps it wasn't far from the truth. I listened to her sobs ease as time went on. Having her in my arms brought forth memories of my mother doing the same thing when I'd been upset and my father worked long hours. She snuck in her own brand of compassion and care without the strict hand of my dad. I relished those times. Stolen moments I'd been able to cry and feel. Her soothing words and gentle touches. Every child needed that, right?

Pulling out of my fierce grip, Char sat upright, wiping her eyes with one hand. "I'm sorry. I didn't mean for you to see me like that."

"Stop. You don't need to apologize. You forget who you're talking to. There's nothing I haven't witnessed." My arms still encased her. She didn't appear in a hurry to move away entirely. "What brought it on?"

Glancing down, she shrugged. "Just sitting around, I guess. Too much time to think. I can't get rid of the sensation of the gun pressed to my head. That stupid piece of metal could have ended it all in a flash."

"I know it's hard. I've had more than my fair share of guns aimed at me, but you have to see the positives. He didn't pull the trigger. He could have, but for some reason, he couldn't do it. You're here and alive. You can't let it destroy you. If you sit around thinking about it all the time, it will consume you."

She stared at me, letting my words sink in. I had more than enough qualifications in the almost getting killed department to be able to advise her and she knew it.

Nodding, she pushed off me and rubbed her face. "You're right. I need to go somewhere. Get out of here. Get my mind off it."

Standing, I gawked at her tight little sleep shorts, which until now hadn't grabbed my attention because I'd been too focused on snapping her out of her stupor. Legs like a giraffe's pulled my eyes south and then north. Her back facing me as she reached into her bag to pull out some clothes, I paused at her ass, all tight and round. A touch of guilt peppered me, thinking sexual thoughts when only minutes ago she'd been a mess on my lap.

My mouth moved before my brain processed the words. "I'm taking you out."

What the hell? I was? Good God. What was happening to me?

It's okay, man. You feel sorry for the woman. Nothing more. Chill.

She spun and glared at me like I'd sprouted horns. "What?"

My eyes found her nipples first. I couldn't help it. They poked through her tight shirt. It took a second before I answered as I swallowed thickly. Red had me all kinds of screwed.

"Ah, you heard me. Get dressed. We're going out."

"You…you…want to go out? With me?"

Sweetheart, with the way you're looking this second, I'd go anywhere. Fuck. Get it together. This is not okay.

"That's what I said. Moving past her, inhaling

something I couldn't pinpoint but which fluttered around my senses, I replied, "Ten minutes. Get ready. Meet me in the garage."

Direct, bossy soldier was back. I had to dig for him and make him cooperate. It's the only way I'd be able to survive the rest of the afternoon and evening.

Chapter Ten

Char

I'd officially turned into the type of woman I swore I never would. Needy. I'd hoped Viper would stay out longer while I cracked under the silence of his home.

And where had the asshole side of him disappeared to? His gentle compassion floored me. The way he held and caressed me. Spoken softly. Who'd have known? I didn't think he had it in him. Mac had told me there was more to the guy than I'd seen, but I refused to believe her.

Could we actually be friends?

I changed quickly, horrified at my reflection in the bathroom mirror. Brushing my hair and tying it up at least made it look half-decent. Washing my face helped, but the puffiness under my eyes remained. Hopefully, we wouldn't be going anywhere I needed to dress up. He hadn't said so.

Reaching for a pair of runners and socks, I was done. I entered the garage and climbed into the waiting SUV.

Buckling up, I noticed Viper had changed too. He now wore a deep green shirt which brought out his eyes, and a pair of black jeans with his signature black boots. He pulled off the look so well, it took me a moment of staring to realize he watched me ogle him, an incline to the corner of his mouth.

Pivoting to face the front, a hot rush blanching my neck and cheeks, I meekly asked, "Where are you taking me?"

Turning the ignition on and easing out of the garage, he answered, "Nowhere you have to worry about too many people."

Attempting to conjure up an image of where I was going, I came up blank, figuring most places had people. Sinking into the seat, I let him take me. In silence, we drove. Funnily enough, it wasn't awkward. We'd come to some form of a truce earlier and it felt…nice.

We didn't travel far. Turning into Matthaei Botanical Gardens, my brows rose in bewilderment. "Out of all the places we could have gone, you brought me to the Gardens?"

Slipping into a parking space, he killed the engine. Angling himself toward me, he shot back, "You have a problem with our town's gardens?"

I couldn't help it. I smiled. For the first time in days. "No. It's just not where I pictured a big, badass soldier would want to spend time."

His face became guarded. "Like I said, you don't know me."

I truly didn't. But I wanted that to change. Keeping things light, not wanting to spoil the mood,

I sang, "Okay then. Let's go immerse ourselves in nature."

His lips twitched. "Let's."

When my hand found the door handle, he ordered, "Don't." Startled, wondering why he didn't want me to get out of the car, I blinked twice, catching his back as he threw back at me while getting out, "I got it."

Well. Things were taking a different turn. Chivalry wasn't dead, and who would have thought a man who had been nothing but mean to me, now offered to open my door. I wasn't about to voice my feminist ways. Let him do it. Rocking the boat when we were sailing nicely wouldn't solve anything.

Opening my door, he lifted his hand to help me out, so I took it. Not needing it, but wanting it. I soaked up what he offered while it lasted.

The gardens were beautiful. Being a weekday, most people were working, so we only had to share it with a few.

Strolling leisurely, we enjoyed the bonsai section before finding a gorgeous rocky pond surrounded by the greenest shrubs I'd ever seen. It was a natural man-made oasis. Immediately I relaxed into the surroundings, feeling my shoulders sag and my breath lengthen.

"It's beautiful. So quiet and peaceful."

Even though the quiet at Viper's house had caused me to go into a tailspin, this was different. I had company, and nature proved once again how powerful it was. Birds twittered and leaves rustled, the sun catching us as it emerged from behind a cloud.

"You've never been here?"

"Not to this part. It was years ago I came. I think I was still a teenager."

"Let's find somewhere we can sit. You want a coffee?"

"Thank you. I'd love one."

Walking down another path, we found a park bench overlooking a larger waterhole.

"Sit and I'll grab the drinks."

Before I could reply he was off. Strange man. Still, this was one of the best things I'd done in a long time. With work taking up most of my life, I'd forgotten to stop and smell the roses.

Only a ten-minute drive from home, I needed to come here more often.

A noise to my right in some bushes made me stiffen. My blood began its loud roar in my ears. For a moment, I'd forgotten about my fears of being alone but suddenly without Viper, I panicked. Spinning around, I searched for the source of the sound, afraid someone would jump from the nearby bushes.

In a second, everything came hurtling back. The gun at my temple. The acrid breath near my ear. The threat of blowing my brains out. Fear rooted me to the spot. Beads of sweat pebbled on my brow. My legs became nothing more than burning pillars as adrenalin heightened. Tears pricked the corners of my eyes and then I realized I was shaking.

Finally, my brain sent a message to my legs and I ran. I needed to leave. Now. Searching the park, I couldn't even remember where Viper had parked.

Paranoia clouded my judgment. What if they'd come back looking for me? To finish me off? What if they'd been watching me all along?

Rounding a bend, twisting to see if I had been followed, I plowed into something hard.

A grunt, followed by "Oooof." And then, "Fuck!"

Jarred from the impact, I latched on to steady myself, realizing I'd crashed into Viper, and he didn't look too happy. A lid had come off one of the coffees he carried and some of the hot liquid had spilled down the front of his shirt, probably scalding him.

"Shit. I'm so sorry!"

"What the hell were you doing? You looked like you had a tornado on your tail."

Feeling suddenly idiotic, I went to reach my hand out to his stained shirt. Why? I had no idea, but gripping it, I pulled it from his ripped abs as if that might stop the burn.

"I…uh…heard something."

He was a statue of godly proportions, all tense and unforgiving. His shirt quickly stuck to his stomach again and as I looked up, I took a step back. Gone was the nice man from moments ago. A hard veneer now coated him. His green eyes, blackened marbles.

"You heard something? Jesus, Red…"

He'd been about to blow his top, but noticing the stray tear which had rolled down my cheek, he let go another curse on the crest of a heavy breath and turned.

"Car. Now."

And so ended the peaceful afternoon. All because I'd freaked out at a noise which had probably been nothing more than a bird.

Hurrying to keep up, I observed his gait. Warrior. He'd switched into the persona that suited him best.

Reaching the car, he handed me the full coffee, walked to a trash bin, downed what was left of his, and threw the cup away.

He stalked to the driver's side. I heard the click of the locks and climbed in, needing the safety of the SUV.

What I didn't expect next was to see Viper pull his shirt off and climb in, throwing the ruined garment into the backseat. Holy hotness. The air had suddenly been sucked from the car. My eyes zeroed in on the red mark caused by the scalding coffee and guilt gripped me.

"We need to go to the drugstore and get some burn cream for that." Gazing up, I collided with fire and ice. His brows drew together and then a smirk formed.

"You think I need cream for a little burn? Seriously? I've been shot, stabbed, starved, and beaten, and you're worried about some spilled coffee?"

Well, I was just trying to help. Nursing experience told me some burn cream would soothe it.

"Fine. Put up with the pain then. I really don't care."

"Oh, you care."

"What?"

Starting the engine, he pulled his seatbelt across his red welt and drove. "You heard me. You care. Admit it." He wolfishly grinned now and I could have slapped him. We were officially back to our bantering. At least his anger appeared to have receded for now. Man, talk about flipping a switch. The guy was all kinds of hot and cold.

Facing the front on a huff, I spurted out, "In your dreams, Rambo."

He laughed. He actually laughed. Hearing it for the first time threw me off. I gaped at him as if he'd just admitted to being half alien. The deep, rather loud rumble filled the car, and before I knew it I was grinning along, unable to help myself.

He slanted me an amused look, lines forming at his temples. It totally transformed his face, and if I didn't know who sat beside me, I'd swear it was a different person. His eyes glinted and his all-American smile warmed me. He became…normal, and not a special, elite soldier.

Realizing he'd made me forget my earlier fear, I turned when he pulled into the garage at his house. I faced him fully. He took a pause as he almost opened his door, waiting for me to say something.

"Thank you," I offered. I meant it.

"For?" His face angled my way.

"For making me forget."

He knew what I meant. I could see it in the depths of two green irises. Almost like someone had done the same for him at some stage. I'm sure they had, given what he'd endured. Presenting me with a quick nod, he exited and I followed, glad we were back home and he was with me. I felt safe. Like having my own personal weapon of mass destruction.

"What do you want to eat, Red?"

Dinner time already? Huh. Not wanting to be a freeloader, I had an idea. "I'll cook."

"You cook?" He balked.

"Hello! How do you think I've survived on my own for so long?"

"Ah, ramen noodles?"

Seizing the dishtowel, I threw it at him. "Jerk."

"That's me." He fished around in the fridge and pulled out a beer. Holding it up, he asked, "You want one?"

A cold beer actually sounded pretty good. "Yeah. Thanks. Now go and do whatever it is guys do so I can cook."

Giving me a precise military salute and a "yes, ma'am," he strolled into the living room.

Chapter Eleven

Viper

Something had shifted. Possibly in the park when Red's panicked body had plowed into mine. Everything in me had fired up on instinct. I'd been ready to murder, but the fear in her eyes had simmered me down. She would be jumpy for a while after what she'd been through, so I needed to respect that. By being a dick to her, it would only serve to screw her up more. I didn't want to be the one to push her over the edge. Never thought I'd say that, but here we were, in my home, me sitting with my feet up, beer in hand, Red in the kitchen as if we were some freaking married couple.

It had been a long time since I'd done…normal. Hearing her rifle through my cupboards looking for stuff made my chest flutter. Taking a long pull from my can, I willed the sensation away. It brought too many hard emotions back of a life I'd been mapping out with the girl I'd loved, only to have it ripped from under me. I couldn't go there again. Wouldn't.

Once Char had recovered, she'd be moving back home and I could get on with things.

Reaching for the remote, my private military cell pealed out, causing me to pause and stiffen. It never rang unless something was going down or Dec was in trouble and needed me urgently.

I kept it on me at all times, so after fishing it out of the pocket of my black jeans, I took a deep breath before answering.

"Go."

Military. Another mission. Leaving in two days. "Roger that."

I sat, taking in the words of my superior. It seemed I was heading back to Afghanistan. Char would need to stay with Mac. The idea of leaving her vulnerable twisted my insides. At the same time, the familiar rush of a battle looming ignited my dark psyche, flooding my brain with endorphins similar to a high. I wondered if Dec got a call. Unlikely, considering his recent near-death experience.

Still, after finishing the military call, I dialed the number on my regular cell, I had to find out for definite. Char needed someone to protect her.

It rang three times.

"Hey bro."

"Hey. How's it going?"

"Good. You? You two murdered each other yet?" His dry chuckle actually served to irritate me for some reason.

"No. Not why I'm calling. Did you get a call from base?"

"Ah, not happening. I lost my military cell when

I ended up bleeding and shot in the alley remember? Besides, I'm still deemed unfit for duty."

Forgetting he'd had it stolen, a quick thought came to me, barreling and picking up speed.

"Jesus!"

"What?"

"That's it!"

"Ah, you're not making any sense, man."

"Your goddam cell. Whoever tried to kill you had your freaking phone. It all makes sense. The reason our men didn't storm the warehouse to help us save Mac. Whoever stole your phone had it that day. My guess is they used it to contact base and call off our team. Shit."

Silence on the other end, and then heavy breathing. "Fuck me. It hadn't entered my head. Now that you mention it, you're right. Didn't you ever follow it up with Sarge, though?"

"He said he'd look into it. Must have been higher up. I didn't get a reply back. Figured he was still attempting to find out what went wrong."

"Let's just hope you blew the fuckers away."

"Yeah, let's hope."

"You never did tell me how you got me out of that situation."

Recalling how I'd sent Mac to the hotel to keep her safe before risking it all to save Dec, I verbalized the memory, perhaps now ready to speak about it.

"I thought you were gone, man. I didn't know how the hell I would be able to take down three armed men on my own and not get shot."

"You've taken down more than that before. I had

faith in you."

"Yeah, but with you it was different. I had more to lose. Plus, I didn't know if they'd called for backup after they left the room. For one of the first times in my life…I was scared. Scared I'd already lost you."

Hadn't that been a fact? It had all but killed me when he'd turned himself over to save Mac. Not that I'd wanted Mac to be killed, but if I had to choose between both of them, it would be Dec every time.

"So how did you manage it?"

"It wasn't as hard as I imagined. Once they had you outside, they let their guards down. Someone had knocked you out, and so two of the assholes had to carry you to the car. I waited until you were in the trunk and made my move."

"Never let your guard down," Dec said as if thinking out loud. It was one of the first things we'd been taught as soldiers and something we'd had to train our minds into. In the zone and focused at all times. When mastered, it was a key weapon in taking down the enemy who weren't trained in mind control. A hard thing to perfect, but necessary to be a cut above the rest. Patience was another taught virtue. Many soldiers struggled with it, but in times of intense watching and waiting for the green light to proceed, it sporadically proved their downfall or death.

"Exactly. Anyway, the rest is pretty self-explanatory. I took one out the second he shut the trunk, and in the blink of an eye the other two had bullet holes in their heads."

"Nice. Thanks, dude. I really mean that. I'd be dead now if it weren't for you."

Taking in a lungful of air, happy with the outcome, not wanting to think of the alternative, I changed the subject.

"Anyway, I'm heading out in two days. Going back to Afghanistan. I hoped you were staying behind. I need you to keep an eye on Char while I'm gone."

"Yeah? Awesome, man. Good to know one of us will be over there kicking butt. Don't worry about it. Mac and I will make sure she's safe. How is she?"

"Not good. Freaking out at the smallest things. Took her to the park today and something scared the hell out of her."

"Sounds like you actually care."

Care? Hardly. I didn't care for much, although Red had grown on me since I'd had to bring her back from the brink of a breakdown more than once. I knew the gutsy woman had balls, so to see her so timid and afraid worried me. I wasn't sure if that was the same as caring, but I sure as shit hoped not, because I didn't really need any extra emotional weight dragging me down.

"Nah. Just doing my job like you asked. Keeping her safe and all that, so I'll need you to take over when I leave."

"Done. Just make sure you come back in one piece."

"You know it." Hearing a sound behind me, I turned and noted Char standing three feet behind me, her brows drawn in. Not sure how much she heard, I said to Dec, "Gotta go, man. I'll call you when I'm ready to head out."

"Stay safe, brother."

Ending the call, I rose from the sofa. Before I could speak, Red began.

"You're leaving? In two days? How long have you known? Were you going to tell me?"

Her voice had risen, fright etched into her face. I didn't know whether to move forward or remain where I was. I chose the second option. She'd obviously heard most of my conversation.

"I only just found out. Another mission came up. Dec will keep you safe."

Initially, she'd wanted to stay with them but now, the look on her face told me otherwise.

"Ahh, I thought you'd be happy. You didn't want to stay here, remember?"

She blinked, looked down at the floor, and then hooked me with her stunning eyes. "I guess…well…it's not as bad here as I thought. I'm just shocked you're going into battle again."

She turned her back on me and strode into the kitchen. Damn it. Following, I saw she'd dished up some chicken and made a salad. Dinner could wait. I needed to clear the air.

Striding closer to where she had stopped with her back to the sink, feeling my body burn the closer I got, I stood toe to toe, peering down at her. "You don't want me to go?" My voice sounded odd. As if a morsel of hope clung to it. Hope that she'd say, "don't go," but she didn't. Instead, she pursed those damn, adorable lips and found her backbone.

"I didn't say that. You think I don't want you to

leave? Please! That's crazy talk. Of course I'll be happy to go with Mac. You just threw me, that's all. I mean, I didn't think I'd be leaving quite so soon."

Yeah. She had unspoken words in that sentence. I wasn't stupid. Her eyes said things she couldn't.

When her head tilted downward again, I grasped a wad of hair and pulled her face back up. I wasn't done with her yet. For some stupid reason, I needed her to be totally honest with me.

"Red, admit it. You'll worry about me when I'm gone."

"No. I'll be glad to see the end of you."

A fire lit in her gaze, and damn if it didn't stoke my own embers. This was the woman I loved to hate. I could deal with our constant bantering and bickering. It was when she became all soft and vulnerable that I floundered. As broken as she'd been earlier, she still had a kick of fire when she needed it.

Pulling harder on her hair, wondering why she wasn't cowering away from me after her attack, I held firm, not willing to hurt her further. Still, I needed to know what went on in that head of hers.

"You going to tell me the truth?"

Her eyes flashed, cheeks reddening. Moving my face closer, I watched her pupils enlarge. Her breasts heaved, grazing my chest.

"What truth? What are you doing?" she asked, her exhalation catching my lips.

My restraint wavered on a dark edge as adrenalin began its destruction through my body. Like on a mission, I walked into unknown territory, the thrill making me heady.

"You don't want me to leave. Why is that, Red? Answer me, and it better be the truth."

Gasping, she attempted to pull her head free, but I held strong. I had all the control and my psyche cheered.

"Or what?" she challenged.

Oh no. Do not challenge me, woman. I will win. Every. Damn. Time. "You don't want to find out."

But the challenge was already there. Egging me to act. So I did. Without thinking. Pure instinct I knew I'd live to regret.

Dragging her mouth onto mine, my fingers still balling in her hair, I thought I'd combust when I tasted her. Every cell in my body imploded. The kiss had a mixture of anger, frustration, and pure need in it. Her lips parted immediately, asking for my tongue. It knew what to do and found hers without hesitation. A low whine left me in a rush as if relief were the cause, and quite possibly it was. It had been a long time since I'd had a woman, desperate and pliant, clinging to me. Her hands found my shirt and seized it.

I let go of her hair and gripped her head with one hand, the other pulling her in until we were glued together. By God, the frustrating woman felt better than I'd imagined. My body ignored my head's warning to back off. She felt amazing. Better than I deserved, given the way I'd treated her. But hell if I wasn't going to enjoy the sensation for a bit longer. The aggressive assault didn't seem to frighten her. In fact, the noises coming out of her throat told me the opposite. Her lips were a feast and I'd been in a famine. Moist and plump, I fed off her and she gave me what I needed as if she knew.

Her curves made me want to explore, and so I tested the waters, sliding my fingers south to her ass cheek. Oh yeah. Just as I figured. Firm and round, fitting into my large hand as if God himself had crafted it just for me.

The heat was unbearable. My mind was a hazy mess of hormones, my body amped up on repressed sexual tension.

When her hands left my chest and worked their way under my shirt to claw their way up my back, I damn near lost it.

Just the simple touch her fingers elicited on my too sensitive skin had me bite her bottom lip, hard.

A growl left me, a muted sound she captured on a hiss, her lips kneading my own. Hard pebbles pressed into my chest, brushing backward and forward. Letting her head go, both hands gripped each ass cheek. I thrust forward, desperate for friction. Pressure built.

Her ass wasn't enough. I needed more. Her breasts beckoned, and in a nano-second I had a handful of plush flesh, thumbing a throbbing nipple into oblivion.

Pulling back, Char arched her neck and let out a long moan. "Ahhh, yesss!"

Hearing her satisfaction pushed me into the red zone. Her long, elegant neck invited my mouth to a feast of epic proportions, allowing me to nip and suck my way along its length.

And then the unthinkable happened. My acute hearing, no matter that I was in the zone, made me drag myself away and spin when I heard a gasp.

Shoving Char behind me without thinking, ready to go ballistic, I tightened in preparation.

Standing in the kitchen entryway stood Mac and Dec. Mac appeared stunned, her eyes wide, hands around her neck. Dec, the prick, grinned like the ass he was. When the hell had they come in, and why hadn't they knocked?

Breathing out harshly as my shoulders released some tension, I barked out, "The fuck, man? Ever heard of knocking?"

"I did. Hard. You didn't answer, so I tried the door. It was open. Ever hear of locking it?"

Remembering I'd gone to check the mail earlier, I'd left it unlocked. Stupid on my part. Now that I had Red to worry about, I needed to keep it locked for her peace of mind and mine. Normally I didn't worry about it. I could take care of anyone who dared try and step foot in my home without an invite. I guess having her around had me not thinking with a clear head.

Char was a quiet mouse behind me. I could only imagine how embarrassed she was. Needing to get rid of the awkwardness, I asked, "So. This better be good."

Mac attempted to relax, but her eyes kept darting from me to where she knew Char hid.

Throwing a six pack of beer on the table, Dec played it cool. "Thought we'd stop by after Mac's shift and have a drink. Say hi before you leave."

Pivoting to make sure Red was decent, I stepped away, walking over to my friends. Giving Dec a bro hug, seeing the knowing smirk back in place, I leaned into his ear and ground out low, "Wipe that smile, shit for brains. It was a moment of weakness. Nothing more."

He roared with laughter, which pissed me off. Giving him a glare, I rounded on Mac and embraced her with more affection.

"Uh, are we interrupting?" she asked. "'Cause we can come back tomorrow night." Noticing the uneaten dinner on the table, she frowned and glanced at Dec. "They haven't eaten yet. We should go."

"No!" Char and I both confirmed in unison. Looking at her with rosy cheeks, oversized lips I'd been gorging on, and her hair clumped in a mess, my inner warrior high-fived at the fact I'd made her look like that.

Mac walked over to Char and both girls hugged. Something was whispered I couldn't make out, so I left them to it, grabbed my plate and cutlery, and walked into the living room, giving Dec the signal to follow. "Grab me a beer."

Chapter Twelve

Char

I eyed my best friend after she'd hugged me. She stood close with a curious look on her face.

"I take it you're feeling better?" she offered.

Knowing what she referred to, I gripped the edge of the sink where I'd been mauled only moments earlier. I could still taste him. Smell him. Feel him. What had happened to my willpower? And why did I not care if I ever found it again?

"I'm okay. Physically, anyway."

Knowing what was coming, I braced myself. Mac looked to where the guys were as if hoping they were still out of earshot range.

"Soooo…you two have come to a truce?"

"Look, I know what it looked like and what you must be thinking. To be honest, it just kind of happened. One minute he was telling me about his next mission in two days, and then, well…you know the rest. Nothing is going on. I don't know. Shit. My mind is so messed up after the attack."

Giving me another hug, she backed off. "It's okay, sweetie. You don't need to explain. You're both adults. You're both attractive. Single."

Moving to sit at the table, she added, "You don't even have to talk to me about it. Come. Sit. Eat your food."

Deciding I didn't want to talk about what just went down because even I didn't know, I sat.

"How are you feeling, really?" she asked, back to the concerned friend.

"My injuries are healing. I just feel…jumpy and scared, you know? Lost and numb at times." Cutting my chicken, I took a bite.

"It's totally understandable. I can arrange for you to speak to Jen at the hospital."

Jen, the psychologist, mainly helped patients, but I knew she'd squeeze me in for a session if I chose. Did I need to? I wasn't sure.

"Maybe. Just give me a few days."

"Okay. Let me know. How long do you think you'll have off work?"

"They've given me a week, but I'll see how I feel in another couple of days. I may return early. I actually think work will help. I hate sitting around thinking too much. You know I'm not one to sit idle at the best of times."

Nodding, she said, "I do know, and I kind of agree about work keeping your mind busy. I just don't want to see you go back before you're mentally ready."

"I don't know if I'll be mentally ready for a while, but I need to get back."

Hearing the boys laughing in the other room, I

changed the subject. "So. It looks like I'll be living with you for a bit, after all."

Smiling, she cheered, "I'm so excited! We can do girly stuff. Lounge around at night in our PJ's. Bitch about work. Not that we don't do that anyway, but you get the idea. It's going to be fun."

"Yeah, fun listening to you two going for it at night. Seriously, how will I cope with that?"

She smirked slightly, her eyes alight as if thinking about her nightly shenanigans. "I'll talk to Dec and insist he tone it down a bit. You know, play the unstable friend card."

"You think he'll be annoyed I'm staying?"

"No!" she offered immediately. He likes you. He'll comply with my wishes and be on his best behavior if he knows just what you're going through."

Breathing out, I hoped so. I hated intruding on their lives now that they were at a better place.

Needing to ask a question I'd wondered about for a while, I didn't hold back. "How do you do it? I mean, you went through far worse than I did and here you are. Normal. I know you had a few freak-outs and nightmares, but you seem your old self."

Looking pensive, she thought about her answer. "It wasn't easy at first. Har…Dec helped. Damn, I still go to call him Harley. He'll always be Harley to me."

Harley was the name given to Declan when he had suffered amnesia and didn't know his identity. We'd all gotten to know him as Harley. Then when his memories returned, he decided no matter how much he wanted to be Harley, he couldn't. Declan was who he truly was.

"We both went through the ordeal together, and I think because we were both involved, it helped when we talked about it. Dec was great. And you, of course. I'm here for you. Let me know what I can do to get you through it."

Picking at my salad, I smiled at her. She truly was the best. "Thank you. I mean it."

Realizing I ate in front of her, I asked, "You want some of this? I've made plenty of chicken and there's some salad left over?"

"No. We grabbed Subway after work. I didn't feel like cooking and neither did Dec."

"Okay. Well, I'm going to leave this for later. I'm not all that hungry now. Let's go join the men."

Putting my plate in the fridge, I followed Mac into the living room. The boys were sprawled out on the couch, beers in hand, smiling about something we weren't privy to. Mac went and sat on Dec's lap, leaving me uncomfortable as to where to sit. Eying the space beside Viper, knowing it wouldn't be a great idea to be that close, I opted for the single chair on the other side of the coffee table. Far enough away to keep his heat from leaching into me.

I couldn't even look at him after our fiery tryst, so I stayed focused on Mac and Dec, but immediately became keenly aware that he watched me.

"You doing okay, Char?" Dec's concern made me smile. He truly cared.

"Yeah. I'll be fine. I'm gonna go back to work in the next day or so. I need it."

"The hell you are!" rumbled a thunderous boom.

Unable to stop my blood from rising at his commanding tone, I shot him a glare. "I'm going. It's not up for debate. You don't get to dictate to me. You'll be gone, anyway."

He clenched the can so tightly I expected it to spill over under the pressure. Green eyes had darkened. A vein in his neck popped. "You're still recovering! You need to rest."

Mac fidgeted on Dec's lap but she didn't interrupt.

"Resting isn't doing me any good. I need to keep busy. I know what I need!" I almost shouted.

Deep down I knew he was simply concerned and it should have placated me, but when someone tried to tell me what to do, it brought out my stubborn side. I didn't like to be told what to do. Especially by such a commanding man who obviously had issues with being put in his place.

"What you need is to listen to reason. You might think you're ready to return to work, but you're not. You freaked out earlier at the slightest sound. That's not ready to go back to a chaotic hospital where you need your wits about you." His voice was eerily low. He stared me down. Tension filled the room.

Dec cleared his throat. "Ahh, how about we assess the situation in a couple of days? Let's get you settled in with Mac and take it from there." Turning to his friend, he shared, "I'll make sure she's ready, man, don't worry."

Viper didn't waver. Something in that gaze made me take pause. It was more than the need to control.

Sitting underneath I saw fear. Fear for me? Fear that he wouldn't be here to make sure I was okay? I couldn't be sure but, I sighed. Could it be possible that he actually did care about me in his own odd way?

Silently he appeared to be pleading with me.

"What Dec said." I put the burden of the conversation back onto someone else.

It took a few more heartbeats, but finally, Viper looked at his beer before taking a long swig. Very slightly he gave a nod, ending the dialogue. Relaxing slightly, I changed the subject, grabbing Mac's attention.

"So, speaking of work, what's been happening?"

Happy to be free from the spider's web of awkwardness, she proceeded to fill me in on what had been going on, leaving the boys to quietly engage in their own conversation. I couldn't help but notice the way Dec rubbed his thumb up and down Mac's wrist, almost absentmindedly. Like he had to be touching her. She really was lucky. I wondered if Viper would ever be so unconsciously tender and then balked at the thought.

He rarely did tender. He only did fierce. Actually not so true. When I'd had a meltdown in the shower, snippets of his tender side lodged in my brain. But for the most part, he acted all macho and alpha. Not that I'd complained before Mac and Dec had turned up. My mind turned to what would have happened if they hadn't arrived. Would we be in the bedroom right now? He'd definitely proven how turned on he'd been. Oh, God. He wasn't small by any means. My skin tingled and I had to change positions on the chair to push away the images of being taken by the beast of a man.

"Char? Did you hear me?" asked Mac, dragging me to the present.

"Huh? Sorry. What were you saying?" I could feel all eyes on me. Lucky they couldn't see into my head.

"Are you okay? You seemed miles away."

"Oh. Yeah. Sorry." Remembering the last thing I'd heard Mac telling me, I hoped she believed me. "Just trying to picture old Mrs. Morris attempting to chat up Dr. Andrews."

She seemed to buy it. Mrs. Morris had been brought through Emergency two weeks ago with pneumonia. The sprightly eighty-six year old, now in a ward, apparently still attempted to humor staff, in between bouts of coughing. The thought of her flirting with handsome Jace Andrews was particularly funny, considering the fine doctor was gay.

A quick glance at Viper showed me his concern mapped out on his face. Perhaps he thought I was going into another meltdown. Giving him my best smile, I turned back to Mac and made sure to pay attention.

***

After a couple of hours, we bid our friends farewell. Fatigue had me wanting to skip my now cold dinner and just head straight to bed, but I knew I needed to eat, regardless of my appetite, which had waned since being wrapped up in one hardened soldier earlier.

Moving into the kitchen, I pulled the plate from the fridge and ate the salad before reheating the chicken in the microwave. Viper hadn't joined me, which I was glad of. Instead, I heard the shower switch on.

Was he pissed at me for defying his request to take more time off work? Too bad. It was my life and I only had myself to answer to.

Images of a hot, wet body flashed across my vision, causing me to squeeze my eyes tightly to get rid of it. Nope. Didn't work. With the sound of the water forging through the pipes and remnants of him over my skin, I became a hot mess. Normally, I'd be like old Mrs. Morris and flirt my ass off for a one-night stand or quick fling, but somehow with Viper, I knew that even after one round of intense sex, I'd be ruined forever. Ruined for other men. Did he do the casual hookup thing? Or had he sworn off women altogether after his 'almost marriage'?

So many questions. So few answers.

Too tired to overthink anything further, I threw the small piece of chicken left in the trash, rinsed my plate, and loaded the dishwasher.

On autopilot I shuffled down the hallway, almost at my room when the bathroom door opened, leaving me breathless.

Naked, except for a sliver of a towel, stood the man of my fantasies. Literally. In an instant, I was alert and focused. He stopped directly in front of me in a taunting manner and damn if I didn't almost crumble.

Small trickles of water pebbled on his torso, new ones dripping down from his wet hair. Healed scars added to his edge. His chest rose and fell as he stood, motionless and silent. Stealthy. I stepped back, needing room to pass, but he took a step forward. Dear Lord, I felt like the prey of a giant predator. Small and helpless.

Don't look, Char. Don't look. But I'd always had trouble following my brain. I rose my chin to find heaven and hell combined. Heavenly good looks mingled with a fire straight from hell. I was in so far over my head that I decided to stop fighting and just concede.

At that point, I couldn't figure out which part I liked more.

"Tell me, Red. Do you always push people to their limit?"

Only you. Only you. I kept that one quiet. Instead, my mouth moved of its own accord.

"I don't know what you mean."

Gripping the back of my neck, he towered over me. "You know exactly what I mean. I think you like pushing my buttons. I think you get off on it."

He smelled of fresh soap and it looked like he'd had a quick shave in the shower. Earlier two-day growth had vanished, along with my willpower.

"Do you?" he moved his face ever so close.

Lips so fine jutted out at me, waiting for…something. My vision blurred. My ribs ached from my thundering heart. I shrugged.

I swallowed, wishing he'd just put me out of my misery. He had far more restraint than I gave him credit for. Years of military work had paid off, although, by the strain of his neck and the firm grip he had on my neck, I'd say he held on by a thread.

Suddenly empowered by that thought, wanting to push him even further to see when his wall of cool would crumble, I shot my tongue out and swiped it over my top lip, firming my spine, as if having him so close didn't turn me into a pliant minion.

Following the path of my tongue, his eyes narrowed a second after they showed his arousal. I held my breath, waiting for his next move.

With no time to react, his mouth caught mine at the very moment he growled. His pillow-soft lips had all the ferocity of a raging storm, firm and insistent. The hand on my neck rose to the back of my skull, to angle me better.

As if Mac and Dec had never visited, we were back to where we were in the kitchen.

Delving with his tongue, I collapsed into him, unable to remain standing. His other arm came around my waist, anchoring me. I swam in him, neither here nor there, but somewhere in between, immersed in pure sensation.

I let out soft sounds of satisfaction so he amped up his assault.

"Put your hands on me." At his command, I complied, forgetting I didn't like to be bossed around. This was a whole other world of domination.

Ironing both hands flat over his abs and chest, I let them roam where they pleased. Damn, he had a body to die for. I hadn't seen Dec without his clothes, but I couldn't imagine him being as ruthlessly chiseled as Viper. He sucked in air through his nose at my touch as if I stung him, but with our vision still in line, it wasn't pain I saw. Totally the opposite.

"You think you can take me, Red?" he forced out, his mouth moving to the apex of my neck and shoulder, biting just shy of discomfort.

Nothing more than a nod came from me. Instead, I let out a moan as he sucked on a sensitive spot which zapped pleasure hormones through every cell. I became the pleasure and nothing else.

I heard a vague snicker against my skin and then I was lifted off my feet, legs splayed around his waist and we were on the move. His mouth still suckled on the way to his room where he didn't even bother shutting the door.

"One chance only. Do. You. Want. This? I know you're still healing from your assault."

I couldn't have stopped. Not now. No way in hell. "Yes." It left on a breathless *oomph* as we landed on the bed in a maze of limbs. Desperately he ripped my shirt off. A seam tore as he wrenched my arm free. Surveying my cleavage in the scrap of a bra, he smiled, and then looked from my chest to my eyes.

"Fuck, Red. You continue to amaze me."

Chapter Thirteen

Viper

I didn't have a clue what in the hell I was doing. My body craved the gorgeous redhead beneath me. Fumbling for the clasp on her bra, I eventually found it and pulled the hindrance off, revealing two perfect peaches for breasts atop a flat belly. A gold ring jutted from the cute button, causing me to officially lose my mind.

She wanted me. Oh, yeah! Rigid nipples and shattered breathing proved it. It took all my restraint and training as a soldier not to ravage her like a beast and have it all over in less than a minute. Breathing in and out through my nose, I centered myself, relishing in the noises coming from her as I adored her chest. Who would have known, hidden beneath her hospital scrubs and casual clothing, lay a man's wet dream? Now that I'd thrown caution to the wind, I was all in. She writhed beneath me, hurrying me up, but I ignored it, fully in control now.

"What's the matter, Red? You seem frustrated." Biting down on her distended nipple, her cry let me know just how much. Mmm. If she kept reacting like that to my touch, I'd be done before we even got to the good part. Perhaps that would be best. Knock one out and then I'd be good to go for longer.

In the back of my mind, I heard whispers of being gentle. She was still extremely fragile. I'd toyed with the idea of not touching her while she sorted through her emotions, but damned if I could hold back. She had this magnet attached to her that even with my fierce restraint, I couldn't resist. The other part of my brain told me that if she didn't want this, she'd tell me so. Perhaps this was her way of not thinking. Just feeling. Her therapy. I'd give her what she wanted.

Lifting her hips, I chuckled at her need. I loved a woman who could match my own desire in the bedroom, and by the look in her heavy eyes, nails digging into my shoulders as I took my sweet time, nipping and sucking while garnering her reaction, she filled that role perfectly. Who would have thought? I guess it's true about redheads being fiery. Well, I already knew she had a red-hot temper, but never did I guess it would play over into other areas. Damn.

"Viper!" she cried as I bit hard. Her torso rose off the mattress in want, making me snarl in response.

My towel had disentangled from my hips and lay on her thigh, so I wrenched it free, leaving myself totally naked. Rubbing against her, I needed to rid her of the rest of her clothes. With one hand, I undid her button and zipper and then sitting up so I knelt with my knees on either side of her, I dragged her jeans and panties south, revealing smooth, fully shaved skin everywhere. Not a hair to be seen. Moaning at the sight, I stilled, getting an eyeful.

"Red?"

"Hmm?"

"You shave for me?"

"Uh…" She didn't get to answer further because I couldn't resist kissing the baby-like soft skin between her legs. Sweet heaven. She tasted all musky and feminine. A scent I'd been deprived of for too long. Way too long.

Holding her hips down when she bucked upward as my mouth fed off her, I indulged in the delicacy, starved. She lit up like a Christmas tree at my touch, spurring me on. I was lost in my own pleasure while listening to hers.

I shouldn't. I really shouldn't, but hell, I was leaving in two days. Who knew when I'd be back or if I would? I wanted to be reminded of this exact moment while I flew into enemy territory. I wanted to think of it while I slept.

"Yes!' she screamed, rocketing out of the stratosphere as I worshipped her with my tongue. Her cries had my ego smirking and my loins ordering some sort of release.

Lifting myself off her and letting my gaze follow the curves up her body, it fell on her sated expression. Head thrown to the side, slight smile tilting her lips. Eyes gently closed.

Stalking to the bathroom, I fumbled in the

bottom drawer where I knew a pack of condoms lay, untouched. I ripped the box, taking two back into the bedroom. Yeah, two was a little arrogant, but once wouldn't be enough, I could tell.

Climbing up on the bed, I hovered over her. "You with me, Red?"

"Unnnhh."

Nothing more needed to be said. I threw myself into her, getting lost, relishing in the ability she had to help me escape the brain clutter of war. We both needed the escape.

I gloried in her touch and sounds, our bodies fitting together perfectly. She took as much as she gave, making me realize for the first time ever I didn't have to try too hard to please her. She adequately fulfilled all my desires. She had passion and fire, matching me kiss for kiss and stroke for stroke. My hands hooked onto her ass and held on for dear life as she turned us and rode me as if her life depended on it. All the while her mouth ravished my lips and neck, her hands gripping my hair, hard. Just the way I liked it. I caught and held her sensuous eyes, watching the pupils dilate further as she got closer to heaven. I hadn't been to heaven in so long, I knew I wouldn't last much longer. She pulled every morsel of pleasure I had and then some.

I drifted on the tide of euphoria as she came undone around me, causing me to splinter into a million tiny fragments, our pieces combining and falling back into place so that I now carried some of her with me.

How did this happen? It was just a release. Some

fun before my deployment. Right? Why then were pieces of her taking up residence in my heart?

I listened to her breathing as her head lay in the crook of my shoulder, that fiery red mane cloaking my arm. Could I go there again with a woman? My brain said no, but that's not what was leading the race at the moment. I wanted nothing more than to be able to push her away, but she still had a vulnerability about her, even after the amazing sex we'd just shared.

Feathering my fingers up and down her back, I asked, "You okay, Red?"

"Mmm." Again, no words, just sounds.

Laughing, I said, "Is this what I have to do to get you to remain quiet? I'll have to remember that next time you're giving me grief, woman."

She lifted her head and smiled groggily. "I'll shut up forever if you keep that up."

And so I took her mouth and body again, keeping my demons at bay for a short while, falling asleep without nightmares for the first time in years.

Chapter Fourteen

Char

What just happened? How had I slept with Viper? And more to the point, why had I enjoyed it so much? I mean, when I'd first met him I thought he oozed that sexy, badass military guy thing, but when he'd opened his mouth, my ranking of him had gone down dramatically.

Listening to his breath as he slept while I rested my head on his arm, I had all sorts of weird emotions plaguing me. He'd proved every bit the warrior I thought he was in the bedroom, but at the same time, he'd let the rare tenderness show.

He was leaving the day after tomorrow. Going to war. Fighting for his life and others. What if he never made it home? How did I feel about that? Thinking about it made my chest feel raw.

I wanted casual. I hadn't done anything more in ages. Why then did I want to snuggle in bed all day with him holding me? He made me feel safe. Glancing at my watch, the time read three forty-five a.m. I doubted I'd be able to go back to sleep now. Too much ran through my head. I let my eyes roam over his face, so peaceful in sleep. Gone was the hard exterior he always showed the world. Replaced by the true man. I believed when people slept, free of ego, this is who they truly were. Viper looked younger. Happier. I wondered if he was dreaming. And what it was about.

He stirred as if sensing I watched him. He didn't wake though. Instead, he mumbled something, rolled to his side facing me, and threw the arm I wasn't still lying on, over me.

I couldn't move if I wanted to.

I let me eyes drift shut, relishing in the feel of a man's warm body cocooning me, and must have drifted off, because the next thing I knew, the sun was angling through the curtain and the warm mound I'd slept up against had vanished, as if he'd been nothing more than a figment of my imagination.

Sitting up, trying not to let his absence worry me, I rose and walked to the wardrobe, throwing on a robe before shuffling down the hall into the living room.

The smell of coffee hit me, so I followed it into the kitchen. I found Viper, shirtless, wearing only boxers, standing at the stove scrambling eggs. Two mugs sat on the table. I glanced from him to the table, and back again.

His eyebrow rose. "Sleep okay, Red?"

"Yeah. I guess. I woke around three forty-five but ended up falling back asleep. You?"

I knew he'd slept well. He'd barely moved all

night.

"Like a baby, actually. Huh. I never sleep that well. Must have been all the sex." He turned back to the stove, but I didn't miss the smirk on his face. Switching off the gas, he plated the eggs and handed me some.

"Thank you. I'm not used to being cooked for. Especially after…well…you know."

He sat opposite, his large frame blocking my view out the back window. "You're in my home as my guest. What sort of person would I be if I didn't feed you?"

"Still, it's nice to have it done for me."

I could sense a little awkwardness between us and the encroaching silence only accentuated it. Had he regretted it? I sure as hell hadn't.

"So…" I began. "What are your plans for today?"

Chewing a large forkful of eggs, he swallowed, my eyes pausing on that mouth which had ravished me only hours before. A tingle shot down my center.

"I've got some packing to do. Have to call headquarters. I gotta head out to the mall to buy a few things." He watched me intently. "You want to get out and go to the mall with me later?"

Feeling a little like a caged animal, I nodded. "Yeah. That would be great. Thanks. Just let me know when."

"Will do."

More silence. Shit. Talk about the morning after. Having to make small talk wasn't something I'd done much of in the past. The fact that my insides were all over the place and my heart beat furiously had me off kilter. All I could think about was his body and the way it had felt…like steel coated in a softer glaze. I could stare at his torso all day.

"Red?"

"Hmm?"

"You gonna be okay if I go do what I have to do?"

"Yes, of course. I'll be fine."

Had he noticed my fascination with his chest? Or his mouth, for that matter? Gah. I was seriously swooning like a teen. The guy had me all mixed up in my head. Like I didn't know the day or time of year. Seriously, the sooner he went on his mission and I got back to work, the better.

And then a thought hit. I hadn't freaked out since yesterday. I hadn't dwelled on my assault. Viper had taken my mind off it. He'd given me the reprieve I'd needed. He'd been the bandage on my wound. I wasn't sure what would happen when he left, but for the time being, I felt…okay. More than okay.

***

We arrived at the mall at three p.m. I hadn't seen much of him at home, as I'd gone to my room and he'd been busy preparing for his departure tomorrow. As I'd sat in silence, the fears I'd been experiencing surfaced a little. Each time my mind tried to return to the darkness, I pictured Viper's complete surrender to me the night before. I hated that I'd loved it. Something else swam through my blood, something separate from my attack. I felt uneasy about his leaving, and I couldn't be sure if it was that I was going to miss him, or something more. Whatever it was, it sat haphazardly on my chest.

We'd agreed for me to be dropped over to Mac's apartment tonight because Viper had to be out of his house before the sun rose in the morning. Not a word more had been spoken about our tryst other than his mention of sex at breakfast, so I figured maybe it had just been a one-off thing between two people who had chemistry, and who needed the reprieve it brought.

Still, disappointment at that thought weighed me down. Viper must have noticed as we walked through the mall.

"You're quiet," he offered.

"Just thinking."

"About?"

You. I couldn't say that. If he did only want something casual, I didn't want to put pressure on him. He needed his head in the game for what he had ahead of him.

"Wondering if I need to buy anything to take to Mac's." Lie.

He eyed me a moment too long, probably seeing right through me with his military instincts, then he simply nodded and we kept going.

He purchased personal items while I browsed, not really into the whole shopping thing, but it was nice to get out. While he paid for his purchases, I stood outside, people watching. I liked to do it sometimes, wondering what others' lives were like.

What jobs they did. I tried to figure it all out by their appearance. Silly, I know, but fun.

"We need to get you a new cell."

I jumped at his closeness. I hadn't heard him approach.

"There's a store not too far from here. I should be able to transfer my old number, hopefully."

We ambled along the mall to the cell phone store and browsed at the handsets until we were served. I'd opted for another iPhone for its simplicity. Explaining that I'd had my other stolen they set about transferring my old number and getting me set up.

Viper sat patiently, watching the front of the shop as if on guard while I took care of business. After half an hour we were back out in the mall.

"You hungry? Viper asked.

"No. I'm fine. I'll grab something later."

As we approached a drug store, he paused. "I've just gotta grab a couple of things in here and then we'll head home."

"Okay. I'll wait out here."

Eying me as if he wasn't sure whether to leave me or not, he gave a sullen nod and showed me his back.

Odd man. One minute he could be 'almost' sweet and the next he turned back into his snarky self. My emotions tumbled everywhere.

I began people watching again for a while, when suddenly from out of nowhere, I got thrust forward as a guy plowed into me from behind. He was running through the mall with a friend. I felt my balance falter, then I began falling. Slowly, but yet too fast for me to stop it. I tried to correct my balance, but it proved too late. I hit the shiny mall floor with a thud, jarring my already sore arm. Pain seared from my fingers to my shoulder. For a moment I remained still, sore and in shock. My purse strap remained around my shoulder, but the pouch was an uncomfortable lump under me. My spare, tiny purse I'd packed to take to Viper's proved a blessing after my other had been stolen but right now, I cursed it.

A large hand gripped me and pulled me up. "Shit, Red? You okay?"

Viper.

Was I okay? Apart from being startled and in a fair amount of discomfort, I guess so. Bracing myself against him, I turned when the guy who hit me yelled from several yards away. "Sorry, Ma'am."

Viper pivoted, and before I knew what happened, he'd strode toward the guy, pushing people out of the way.

I called out to him, "Viper. It's okay. I'm all right." He either didn't hear me or chose to ignore my plea.

I watched on, helpless, as the guy who rammed me focused on the giant, scary dude who looked like he could blow a gasket at any second. His eyes widened as he turned to flee, but Viper reached him first, gripping the guy's arms to spin him around.

The whole of the mall must have heard the roar. "You! Watch where you're going! You're not supposed to be running inside."

"I'm sorry." The dude looked genuinely

remorseful and I couldn't help feeling sorry for him for being accosted by Viper. At the same time, it appeared as if Viper was protecting me. Again.

"You need to apologize. Properly." He pulled on the guy, whose friend stood on watching, dumbfounded.

People had stopped to stare. They made their way back to me and stood motionless. Viper still had the guy in a firm hold. "Say it to her face."

He looked livid, and I was glad I wasn't the poor guy, who only looked to be in his early twenties…if that.

The guy's cheeks had reddened in embarrassment. "I'm sorry."

"Not good enough!" thundered Viper.

Okay. Now I was getting embarrassed. "It's all right. Really. I'm fine," I offered, hoping to get the guy off the hook.

Viper jerked on the guy's arm to hurry him into his apology.

"Uh, I shouldn't have been running and should have been watching where I was going. I apologize."

"Thank you." I smiled in an attempt to put the poor guy at ease a little.

Viper let go of the guy's arm, which I was sure would be bruised. "Think next time. There's women, children, and elderly in here."

Nodding furiously, the guy waited. Viper ignored him, turned, and came closer to me. "You sure you're not hurt?"

Not wanting to anger him more, I simply said, "Yeah."

Giving the young guy one more heated stare, Viper put his hand in between my shoulder blades and gave me a little shove to move us along, leaving the poor sap standing there, intimidation written all over his face.

When we were exiting the mall, I asked, "Did you really have to embarrass the kid like that? He said sorry."

Stopping, his hand fell from my upper back. "You're seriously questioning why I did that? He pushed you over. You could have cracked your head on the floor. And don't tell me he didn't hurt you. I know you fell on the shoulder you injured during your attack."

His voice had risen. I didn't want to get into an argument but I had to make him see. "Look, I appreciate you defending me like that. I do. It's just that you can't always react with such anger. The guy didn't mean to run into me. He shouldn't have been running inside, no. But I would have just let it go when he said sorry the first time. You caused a scene."

"I'm gonna cause another scene in a moment, Red. Just get to the car."

He stormed off. I followed. Did he not see how flying into a rage over something minor was wrong? Obviously not. It was what he trained for. I guess he reacted without thinking.

When we reached his SUV, he unlocked it and climbed straight into the driver's seat without helping me. Yep. He was pissed.

Pulling out of the parking lot, I trod carefully, but I had to find out what had prompted him to almost lose it.

"Why did you react the way you did?" Sneaking a peek sideways to garner if he would chew my head off, I watched the way he heavily shifted the gears and gripped the wheel. His jaw was locked.

He breathed in and out through his nose, not looking my way. He didn't answer right away, and for a moment I thought he would ignore me, so I glanced out the side window.

Then he spoke. "After what you went through with your mugging, when I turned and saw you on the ground, I acted on instinct. I thought someone had purposely set out to hurt you."

I understood his logic. Being who he was, he didn't think first.

"Thank you. I mean it. I just feel sorry for the poor guy. Did you see his face when you stormed toward him?"

Sliding a half-smile my way, his eyes crinkled. "He about crapped his pants."

"Hahaha. Yeah, he did. And so did his friend."

"Well, they won't forget it in a hurry. Lesson learned, hopefully."

Even though I didn't like the way he went about handling the situation, I had to laugh some more. Now that I knew Viper more intimately, he didn't come across as such an intimidating ogre but looking at it from a stranger's point of view—very much so.

My new cell pealed out. Digging it out of my purse, I checked the screen. Mac's number.

"Hey, girl. How's work?"

"Busy as usual. I'm on my break. Just wondering

if you wanted me to pick you up after I've finished. That way it will save Viper a trip over."

It would mean spending less time with him. A pang of sadness filtered through my chest. I'd been hoping to go to Mac's later in the evening so I could have dinner with Viper. Like the last supper. Silly really, but I wasn't sure how long he'd be away. Nausea swished heavily in my gut at the idea of him being in a war zone. We weren't even an item. We weren't really anything and my nerves were in the red zone. How did wives or girlfriends cope?

"Char?"

Oh. Mac waited for an answer. Not wanting to disappoint her, I said, "Yes. That would be fine. I'll pack up my stuff this afternoon and be all ready for you."

"Great. I'll pick up a bottle of wine on the way home. You up for some Subway for dinner?"

Mac's go-to meal. "Sure. Grab me a BBQ chicken sub."

"Awesome! I've just been paged so I gotta go, but we'll catch up later. Can't wait to see you."

"Me too."

After hanging up, I wondered if Mac would notice I'd slept with Viper without me having to say anything. Would it be written on my face? Could I hide it, and more to the point, did I want to? Hell, I needed to tell someone. Maybe after a couple of glasses of wine, I'd confess my sins and be done with it. I wondered what her reaction would be. Would she be happy I'd officially ended my dry spell or would she be worried I'd slept with a man who may not return from war? No. I didn't think she would be like that. After all, she'd snagged her own soldier.

I could feel Viper's questions without him having to ask them.

"Mac's picking me up on her way home from work so you don't need to worry about taking me over."

"Oh. Cool. You want to go home and pack?"

It's not like I had much to throw in my bag. Clothing and toiletries. I really needed to go to my apartment and grab some more. I hadn't wanted to because of what happened there, but with Viper at my side, perhaps I could do it.

"Would you mind dropping by my apartment so I could grab another bag of stuff?"

He swung his surprise my way. "You okay to do that? I mean the whole reason you've been staying with me was that you didn't want to go there after what went down."

I didn't want to, but hell, I'd have to return there eventually. And it would only be for a short time. I'd get in and out as quickly as possible.

"Yeah. If you don't mind going inside with me."

He glanced back to the road, his jaw muscles working before he looked at me again, his eyes softer. "Sure. Let's head there now."

Switching his indicator on, we turned around at the next intersection and drove to my apartment without speaking.

Images of that fateful night slid across my mind in bursts. I recalled how terrified I'd been, not knowing if the guy would pull the trigger. Each second he didn't was a blessing.

Pulling up to the curb outside my place, a shiver plated goosebumps all over. I took a deep breath and just sat there, picturing myself with the metal barrel pressed to my temple.

A hand touched my arm. "You sure you want to do this?" His voice held understanding. "You want me to go in and grab a suitcase full of clothes for you?"

Flitting around at his unexpectedly kind offering, my insides warmed. He would do it if I agreed. No questions asked. That's the type of guy he was. Knowing that, I shook my head.

"No. I'll do it. Just stay close."

Getting out of the car, he strode around to my side while I collected myself. Reaching out, I took his hand, the size of it alone bringing about some strength. He wouldn't let anything happen to me.

I let him lead me up to the porch. We stopped and he looked at me. I realized he waited for my keys, so I pulled them out of my purse, I handed them over, looking all around as if one of the guys would appear suddenly again.

A slight creak of the door had me pushing up against Viper's back as he stepped over the threshold. Even inside, I expected an intruder to be lurking, so I gripped his shirt and held on as I stared at the floor where I'd fallen and lain in a heap. I took in a large gulp of air as I stepped over the spot. Pausing, he peered over his shoulder. "You want me to carry you, Red?" I didn't miss the sarcasm. If I was any closer, he'd be giving me a piggyback ride.

My chest felt small, my airways narrowing with each step we took deeper into the living room toward the hallway.

"No." It didn't sound very convincing, but I had to do this. I couldn't let a stranger alienate me from my own home. It was a one-off occurrence. Robberies happened all the time.

"Which bedroom is yours?" he asked.

"Last on the right," I mumbled, the tiny hairs on my arms standing on end.

There were only two bedrooms, so it wouldn't be hard for him to work out which one was mine. The other room had a single bed, whereas mine had a queen.

It felt weird being home and even weirder with Viper in it.

We made it without being accosted. I quickly moved to my walk-in closet and found my suitcase leaning up against the wall.

Get in and out. That's what I needed to do. My breathing had calmed but I wasn't comfortable.

Lifting a handful of clothes, hangers included, off the rack, I didn't care what I grabbed. I just stuffed them in the case without bothering to neatly fold. Stepping out into my room, I caught Viper looking at a photo of me on the nightstand. It was one of my favorites, taken in California on the beach. I was soaking wet, standing in the knee-deep surf and just happened to glance up when my then boyfriend, Jason Roberts, had clicked the candid shot. We'd dated five years ago for a year and had gone on a long weekend to Cali. I'd been happy at that time. Carefree. Much like I'd been before my attack. It showed in the picture. It was one of the very few long-term relationships I'd had.

He glanced sideways and cleared his throat, aware I'd caught him staring before he sat on my bed while I proceeded to take my lingerie out, carefully bundling it into a ball so he couldn't check out what I wore. He appeared nervous to be in my space, or maybe it was just the fact that he knew what I held.

Lastly, I got some more makeup out of the bathroom and jammed it all into the overflowing suitcase, barely able to do it up as it bulged at the seams.

"Done. You ready?" I asked, admiring the view of a large tank of a man on my bed. I'd barely had a handful of men in it since I'd been single. Not that I hadn't gone on plenty of dates. I just hadn't brought many home.

Standing, he took a step toward me and stopped. He opened his mouth and then shut it again.

"What?" I asked.

Shaking his head slightly, he took me in before saying, "You did good. Coming here, I mean. You're stronger than you give yourself credit for."

What was that in his eyes? Respect? Awe? I couldn't tell, but hearing his praise steeled my determination.

Seeing my bag at my side, he moved to grab it, his hand grazing mine as he clutched the handle. Our eyes clashed for a long moment, both of us feeling the draw. The pull. He looked away first and turned, dragging my suitcase behind him. "Grab anything else you need and I'll meet you at the car."

I followed him out, disappointed he'd dismissed our connection, wondering if there would be anything in the kitchen I needed, but decided against it. I had plenty of money in the bank. I'd buy food for Mac as long as I stayed with her.

Shutting and locking the front door, a sense of sadness weighed my shoulders down that I'd be living away for a bit. Normally I loved my home. My space. Now it felt invaded and I couldn't help but feel it would never be the same again.

Chapter Fifteen

Viper

She damn well had me at hello. Not that I'd let on how I felt anytime soon. Her continued strength, a quality in a woman I admired, blew me away. Just now, in her home, I'd expected her to crumble. She hadn't been comfortable, that had been obvious, but it hadn't got the better of her. Perhaps my presence had helped, but still, I knew how shaken up she'd been.

Red would be okay while I was away. She'd carry on with life and survive. I didn't know what we were doing after sleeping together, but the thought of not seeing her for the next few weeks, maybe months, left a certain amount of unease behind my ribs.

Could we be more than a casual hook up? Glancing over at her sitting in my passenger seat, I couldn't deny what a firecracker she was in the bedroom. Hell, it had been using all my restraint not to accost her today. Sleeping next to her had kept my nightmares at bay. Another first. She got under my skin more than just physically, though. She had spunk and fire. I liked that. I liked that a lot.

She must have sensed me watching her because she turned and gifted me with her stunning eyes. They crinkled slightly, causing a zing from my heart to my groin. Turning back to the front, I had to swerve sharply to avoid driving onto the gravel on the side of the road.

"Jesus." It came out as a quiet curse from her. "Can you watch the road, instead of me?"

Caught in the act. I didn't know how to respond to that so I used the coping mechanism I knew well. Sarcasm.

"Don't flatter yourself, sweetheart. Not everything's about you."

I regretted it the minute it came out. Fact of the matter—I had been staring at her. I'd been doing it more and more. Not to figure her out, but to figure out the jigsaw puzzle of my emotions while in her company.

"Fuck you." Her voice held some of the fire I'd witnessed when we'd first met and damn if it didn't have me grinning like an idiot.

"Oh, you think it's funny, do you? Being an ass. Here I thought you were actually beginning to treat me like a human. I guess now that you got your end in, it's back to the way things were. Nice."

Peeking sideways, the hurt on her face got my attention before she quickly shuttered it away, replacing it with the brave mask I was beginning to recognize. I felt like a dick. She'd been more than a quick roll between the sheets, as much as I hated to admit it. But my stubbornness thwarted me telling her how I felt. I'd be gone tomorrow. No sense in making promises I wouldn't be able to keep. Friends I could do. Anything more wasn't guaranteed.

I kept my mouth shut the rest of the way home for fear of saying something I'd regret. Drama would serve no purpose to me in the coming weeks. My head had to be back in fight or flight mode, not worrying about a sexy-ass woman and whether or not she meant anything serious or not.

Once home, I made a beeline for my room, closing the door so I could breathe properly. I needed to pack, and doing so now would give me something to focus on other than fighting to keep my hands off the redhead in my kitchen one last time before deployment.

My huge army duffel burst at the seams after throwing everything I needed into it. An hour had passed, giving me a reprieve. Seeing my gear and weapons had me psyched for what lay ahead. A thrill worked its way into my blood.

I could practically smell gunfire mixed with the rocky, mountainous dirt. The adrenalin that kicked in on the flight into enemy territory, not just mine, but the whole team. It would be weird going in without Dec this time, but I was happy he remained safe at home.

Checking I hadn't forgotten anything, I returned to the living room to find it empty. Checking the kitchen, it too remained quiet. Grabbing a beer, I sat on the sofa and flicked on the television. I just began to immerse myself in a NASCAR race when soft feet padded down the hallway. Red moved into my line of sight, changed into a skin-tight pair of jeans with a tank. I couldn't stop staring at her ass, knowing I'd had my hands all over it the night before. I knew what lay beneath the dark-wash denim. I barely saw her place two large bags beside the door. All I could see were two perfect globes, tightening as she bent lower. My crotch stiffened immediately. Eying a cushion beside me, I threw it over my growing erection and turned back to the TV, pretending I hadn't been having dirty thoughts.

"I'll be out of your hair soon. It's four o'clock. Mac will be here in a bit."

"You gonna be okay? With Mac?" I knew she would, but a part of me wished I could stay and make sure.

Slanting me confused eyes, she asked, "Why wouldn't I be?"

Because Mac can't keep you safe like I can. I didn't voice it out loud. With any luck, Dec would be around there all the time.

Shrugging, I let my eyes say what I couldn't. "Just want to make sure."

She stared for a moment too long, allowing me to see behind the mask she wore. A vulnerability brought on by the attack still had her doubting leaving. Perhaps not just because I could protect her. She felt something for me. Whether it simply be sexual attraction, I couldn't be sure, but she'd allowed me to see her at her worst, not necessarily intentionally, but to share that with someone almost always changed the dynamics of a relationship.

Moving to the other end of the sofa, she sat.

"You all ready to leave early in the morning?"

Small talk was better than no talk. Taking a swig of my beer, I relaxed a little. Soon we'd be parting ways and would probably not have much more to do with each other. Life would return to normal. I could handle another hour or so of chitchat.

"Good to go." What more could I say? I could feel her warmth reaching out to me in stark contrast to the cold beer I held.

"Will we hear from you while you're away?"

"Nope. No contact whatsoever."

"Oh."

She fidgeted, crossing her legs and twisting her fingers on her lap.

Sighing out, I offered, "Don't worry. I'll be fine. I've got an elite team and state of the art equipment."

I found the stormy sea of her eyes, wishing I hadn't. A shooting jolt of electricity speared into my torso. It almost broke some of the steel around my heart. I faltered with my bottle to my mouth, needing to say something else to erase her worry.

"Dec will keep watch over you. Make sure you're safe."

"It's not that…"

Placing my beer on the coffee table, I pivoted, bending my right knee so I could face her. "Then what is it?"

"I…it's just…I don't want anything to happen to you. You say you've got a great team, but you can't know what dangers are lurking."

"You're right. I can't. But I'm highly trained. My senses are perfectly honed. I know what I'm doing."

She really appeared rattled. Her face still held doubt. What could I do to make her believe? I lived for war. I was made to be a soldier.

Before I could utter a sound, she spoke. "How do you do it? Go fight, knowing you might not make it back?"

How did I do it? I really didn't know. "Ahh, I'm not sure. I don't really think about not coming back. I do what has to be done to help keep the world safe. I guess my brain is wired differently than others, but it has to be. If I freaked out over there about dying, I probably would get killed by not paying attention."

"So…dying doesn't bother you?"

Okay, this was a weird conversation.

"No. To be honest, living scares me more at times." Truth. In combat, I felt comfortable. At home, I struggled.

"Hmm," was all she murmured.

"What?"

"It's not uncommon for soldiers to feel that way. Civilian life is hard. War changes people. Those close to you may not understand."

"And you do?"

"Are you saying I'm close to you?"

I'd thrown myself into that one. "I'm not saying anything. I'm wondering how you know so much about what soldiers feel."

"I'm a nurse. I've dealt with PTSD."

Rubbing a hand over my face, I exhaled loudly. "And? What were your findings?"

"Exactly what I just told you. For many, they

can't take *normal*. They would rather be at war."

She'd hit the nail on the head. That's exactly how I felt, even though I didn't want to. Did she really understand what it was like, though? How could she? You had to be inside one's head to truly grasp the mental fuckery. But maybe having someone who had dealt with it…no. Don't go there. She'll forget all about you when you're gone and move on.

A car sounded outside and then a door shutting. Footsteps coming up the front steps. Knocking.

I looked at Char.

"That'll be Mac." Glancing at her watch, she added, "Well, she's early."

On instinct, I rose and flew toward her. "Wait. I'll get it."

She spun, wide-eyed as if to ask why.

"You said it could be Mac, but she's early. How often does she finish early at the hospital?"

Watching, recognition set in, she nodded at me and looked at the door.

After everything that had gone down, I wasn't taking chances this close to my leaving.

Swinging open the door, shoulders squared, I relaxed when a smiling Mac stood there in her scrubs.

"Hi, Viper. How's things? You all ready for tomorrow?"

Letting go of my soldier, I offered her more of the real me, smiling back. "Hi, Mac. Yeah. All set. Come on in."

I liked her. She was cool. More importantly, she could handle Dec, which held her in high regard with me.

"Hey, girl. You're early. That's rare." Char was hugging her friend.

"I know, right? One of the quietest afternoons on record. I mean, that's good. It means no one is injured, sick, or worse, but yeah, it was actually weird. They sent me home an hour early."

"Make the most of it when you get it," Char answered, moving to pick up her two bags.

I couldn't let her carry them. My mother had taught me better than that. "Here. I'll get them."

"Oh. Thank you."

Our gazes locked. This was it. The defining moment. She was leaving and so was I.

The front door still sat open, so I moved away and out, peeling my eyes away. It was harder than I thought now that the moment sat heavily upon us.

The two girls followed me to Mac's Mustang. She walked to the trunk and unlocked it, allowing me to put the bags in and shut it. My stomach churned with what? Nerves? Strange. I could go into battle without a flutter and here I stood, awkwardly not knowing what to say to a woman who appeared just as nervous. Her fidgety eyes caught mine and then the ground.

Mac cleared her throat and offered, "Okay. Well, you stay safe, you hear? We want you home in one piece." She walked to me and wrapped her arms around my neck. I hugged her back, taking in a large breath when she whispered, "Don't worry. We'll look after her."

I knew Red would be in good hands, but looking at her now, she seemed like a lost lamb and a small amount of guilt rode my tail.

Her chin rose in that defiant way I'd come to know and like. "So…I guess you finally get rid of me, huh?" The smile wasn't genuine.

"I guess so." I regretted it before it even came out. "I mean, you look after yourself and keep Mac and Dec close."

"Is that an order, soldier?"

"Damn straight it is." My throat locked up. Her fiery curls were loose and flowing gently in the slight breeze, her green eyes, catching the afternoon sun, appeared almost incandescent. God, she looked stunning. Mac was in the driver's seat and had cranked the engine, the beefy sound spurring me on to say goodbye.

"Uh, you gonna be okay?" I asked, stepping into her so we were almost flush.

Her head rose to look at me. I caught her glassy stare. She was about to cry. I caught her large swallow.

"Yeah. I'll be fine. Don't worry. Just go and focus on your job."

My hand lifted without me willing it to. I needed to feel her soft cheek. To memorize it into my psyche for the dark times coming.

"I'll see you when I see you, Red."

She nodded, her bottom lip shaking. I decided at that moment that I'd regret it if I didn't do it, so I slammed my mouth onto hers, not in an open-mouthed, passionate kiss, but a closed mouth goodbye-type of kiss. Her lips were soft and pliant, and it wouldn't have taken much to have her yield to me. Fighting off the need, I pulled away and said more sternly than I wanted, "Go!" It was an order. She needed to leave so I could shut down the strange fluttering that had now grown into a sensation much larger. My heart thundered.

I couldn't watch the car leave. I couldn't let her forlorn face be the last thing I saw of her.

Striding toward my front door, I walked inside, slamming it behind me. Jesus! Why did I feel like I'd just let the best thing to ever happen to me drive away?

Chapter Sixteen

Char

"Okay, what was that?" Mac asked as soon as we pulled away from Viper's house.

"What are you talking about?"

"You know what. Don't act all innocent to me, missy. There were some serious vibes going on back there."

She could read me like a book. I hadn't told her about sleeping with Viper yet but apparently, it was written on my face. After she and Dec caught us making out in his kitchen, I was surprised she even asked.

Glancing tentatively at her, I sucked in a breath and blurted out, "We kind of had sex."

Hitting the brakes and pulling into the curb she squealed, "What? Oh, my God. I knew it! When? How?"

"I think you know the how's of it all but it happened last night."

"Ha! You're funny. I want details!"

"Fine, but can you keep driving while I tell you?" It would be easier to tell her while she wasn't looking at me. I wasn't going to share all the sordid details but simply gloss over them.

Easing back onto the driving lane, I began, "It kind of just happened."

"Uh huh. From where I was standing in the kitchen when we arrived, I'm not surprised you needed to finish what you started."

I ignored that. "Anyway, I was in the hallway, and he came out of the shower…"

"Naked?"

"No. Well, nearly. Just a towel."

"Ooh, is he as ripped as Dec?"

"I haven't seen Dec naked, but I'm guessing so."

Mac's eyes twinkled at the mention of her man. "Oh trust me. He's lethal."

We both laughed and suddenly I relaxed more. I got the impression Mac wanted to see Viper and me together. Or else she just wanted him to settle down.

"You still want Subway for dinner?" she asked, changing the subject.

"Of course." I hadn't really eaten much apart from the big breakfast, so my stomach rumbled from starvation.

Arriving at Mac's with our food, my nerves kicked up again. Dec's truck was parked in the visitor's bay a couple of doors down.

It would be weird with him there all the time. Not that I didn't like him, but I'd be the third wheel.

"I'll get Dec to grab your bags. Let's go eat."

She led the way, pushing through the front door. Dec had just stepped from the hallway into the living room. As soon as he made eye contact with Mac, his expression changed from pensive to almost euphoric. It was actually sickening. His whole face crinkled when he smiled, and his eyes held more than just excitement to see his girl. Love. So much love. I could see it as plain as day. Mac dropped her purse, the Subway bag and the wine she must have bought before picking me up, and almost ran to him. He picked her up, pressing her to him and kissed the hell out of her.

Okay. Definitely the third wheel here. I glanced away, uncomfortable.

Mac pulled back as Dec rumbled, "I missed you, angel. How was work?"

"I missed you too. And work was quiet."

"Huh. It happens, I guess." He placed her feet back on the ground before he realized I stood a few feet away.

"Char. Good to see you."

I admitted to myself his smile would make any woman swoon. One couldn't help but smile back.

Striding forward, he embraced me in a rib-crushing hug. "You've come to join the funny farm, huh?"

"Hey!" Mac responded, not angry. More amused. "Speak for yourself."

Whispering in my ear before he got a swipe on the rear he said, "Don't listen to her. She's crazy."

"I heard that!" He flinched, then laughed when he received the swat on the butt.

He appeared to be doing a lot better now after his run-in with death. Twice. He was the happiest I'd known him since his full memory returned. I credited a lot of it to Mac.

"Ow, woman! You've got a mean backhand."

"Good, now please go and get Char's bags out of the trunk and put them in the spare room."

Giving her a two-fingered salute, he offered, "Yes, ma'am."

When he walked out, I said to my friend, "You've got him tied around your little finger."

"Hahahaha! Right? It's not intentional. He just happens to adore the ground I walk on."

"You're lucky, you know?"

She gave me a look that told me everything. "I know. It hasn't been easy, though. In fact, it's been damn hard, as you are well aware of."

"Yeah, but it's been worth it. I've never seen the two of you so happy."

"You'll find it too. Don't worry." Winking, she walked to where she'd dropped the sandwiches and wine and headed into the kitchen. "Do you want a plate for your sub?"

"Please. And a wine would be great."

"You got it. Sit and make yourself comfortable."

I'd no sooner sat down than Dec bounded through the door with my bags. On his way to my room, he asked, "How's my boy? He raring to go?"

Viper. "Ah, yeah. He actually is."

Hearing him open a door and place the bags on the floor, I waited for him to return.

"Don't take it personally. It's a soldier thing."

"He tried to explain it to me."

He sat on the other side of the sofa. "He'll miss you. That's a fact."

"Oh. I don't really think he will." *Would he?*

He tapped on his nose. "Instinct. Trust me. You got to him. I know my friend."

My neck heated. Were they really that close that they could sense things so personally?

"Did he say anything to you? About me?"

"He didn't have to. I observe. Not to mention what we walked in on." His voice had lowered as if he didn't want Mac to hear him mentioning it.

Embarrassed at being caught, I shot up from the couch. "I'll just go and see if Mac needs a hand."

I heard his chuckle all the way into the kitchen.

Chapter Seventeen

Char

Hours turned to days. Days into weeks. Three to be exact. Three long weeks of work and sleep with small amounts of food in between. I missed him. At night in bed, my mind began its cruel torture of imagining him hurt or worse. I hated not knowing. Dec hadn't heard either.

Living at Mac's had its advantages. Company, for one. If I'd been at my apartment, alone, I'd surely have gone stir crazy by now. Even with my hectic schedule. On days off, Mac made sure we remained busy.

It was Sunday morning, early. I hadn't slept well. I'd had a weird feeling most of the night I couldn't explain. Uneasiness, I suppose could best describe it. Just the sensation of something not being right. After fruitlessly attempting sleep but doing nothing except tossing and turning, I got up and now sat in the kitchen at Mac's with a steaming mug of coffee in my hand, hoping it would dispel the disquiet.

Movement to the side had me look up, catching sight of Dec. He smiled and rubbed at his eyes before spying the freshly brewed coffee pot.

"Couldn't sleep?" he asked, wearing only boxers. I'd had to get used to his half-naked body around all the time because when he was here, he always seemed to be shirtless. Not that I minded. He was all kinds of hot. But he was very much my best friend's, so I kept my thoughts to myself. Besides, Viper had wormed his way under my skin and appealed to me way more.

Shrugging, I sipped my brew. "Nah. You?"

Pouring his coffee, he sat opposite. "Comes with the territory. I have nights where I don't get any, and others where I sleep like a rock. Having Mac next to me helps." His eyes crinkled when he said my friend's name. He loved her so much.

Suspicion clouded his eyes. "You okay? You seem to have settled in here really well. You seem…happier. Why the restless night?"

Dec was easy to talk to. Sometimes I felt better talking to him than Mac…just to have a male perspective on things. Mac had a way of getting me to bare my soul at times, but with Dec I didn't need to.

"I'm not sure. I began feeling unsettled before I dozed on and off. It stayed with me all night, and even now, I can't shake it, you know? I just hope Viper is okay."

His right eyebrow rose into his growing fringe. Since I'd moved in, his hair had grown out, curling slightly at the ends. "You're worried about Viper?"

"Aren't you?"

Swigging his caffeine, he looked down at the table, then back up at me, taking a deep breath.

"Well, yeah. I mean, I guess. It's not something I dwell on, but then, I've been where he is now. I've lived it. It's a job. I know how capable he is, so I don't think about it too much."

Just then Mac appeared in her tank and sleep shorts, eyes half-closed. "What are you guys doing? It's six o'clock on Sunday." She walked to Dec and placed her arms on his shoulders, standing at the back of his chair.

"We both couldn't sleep. I got up and smelled coffee, so it led me blindly to the kitchen." Dec touched both of Mac's hands affectionately. God, I wished I had what they had.

I looked away because of the twinge of jealousy that reared its head. They both deserved all the happiness in the world after they'd fought so hard to be where they were today.

She leaned down and kissed his head, then went and poured her own cup. "Well, I'm up. Might as well join you guys."

Dec piped up, "So, are we still on for the Street Art Fair today?"

We'd agreed to go to the week-long street art fair today. It was held every July in Ann Arbor. A great way for local artists to display and sell their wares. I'd always loved arts and crafts but had always been too busy with my career to dabble. Getting to browse and purchase others' masterpieces was the next best thing.

Glancing at Mac, she nodded, knowing how

much I'd been looking forward to it. "Hell yeah. Wouldn't miss it."

***

At ten o'clock we were wandering amongst some of the region's finest artists and their creations. I felt in my element. I'd forgotten about the creepy, anxious sensations plaguing me and reveled in the color and ingenuity of the stalls. Music could be heard from a stage nearby, and the atmosphere was electric. Dec had bought us all coffees as we carelessly strolled and chatted, remarking on beautiful items and the more eclectic ones. A charming piece caught my eye. A gem in its own right, I stopped at a handmade jewelry stand. Hanging in front of me with the sunlight catching it sat the most beautiful amethyst necklace I'd ever seen. Masculine in its appearance, it hung on a black cord and had two metal squares similar to dog-tags on either side. I had to get it for Viper. The oval polished amethyst had healing qualities to help reduce stress, anxiety mood swings, and other mental issues. I figured it might help Viper sleep at night and his PTSD.

Picking it up, I let it sit on my palm, feeling its texture and weight. Something drew me to it, whether it was the stone itself, or the significance of the design, I couldn't be sure.

"It's a lovely piece, that one," the smiling woman, serving, said.

"It is. Do you make all these yourself?"

"Yes.

"They're gorgeous. I've never seen anything quite like this before." I held up the necklace. Mac and Dec had stopped and backpedaled to stand by my side.

"Wow. I love it," crooned Mac, moving in for a closer look. Grinning, she lifted her gaze to mine. "I'm gathering it's not for you?"

Shaking my head, I didn't need to say anything. It was obviously a masculine piece.

"I'll take it." Giving it to the lady, I pulled a fifty dollar bill from my purse and handed it over. She placed it in a small black pouch and gave me ten dollars change.

A small price to pay for something so extraordinary. I wasn't sure when I'd be able to give it to Viper, but buying it and keeping it fortified in my mind that he had to return home now to accept his gift. Kind of like a good omen.

Dec stayed quiet about the purchase. I didn't know what he thought about me purchasing it for his friend, but I didn't care.

We strolled around the rest of the exhibits and before we knew it, lunchtime had rolled around. My loud, rumbling stomach let it be known how hungry I had become.

"You up for some cool vegetarian food?" Mac queried.

"Since when have you ever turned away from meat?" I knew she liked a good steak like the rest of us.

"I'm not fully vegetarian, but I've been thinking of it for a while now. Come on. There's a great little café just up ahead. It serves the best food you will ever have."

Tagging behind, I pulled out the necklace again, turning it beneath my fingers. I hoped he liked it. If not, I'd have to find someone else to give it to.

A cell pealed out, and at a quick glance, I could tell it was Dec's.

He stepped away, checking the screen, answering in a low voice.

I looked at Mac and she simply said, "One of Viper's private phones he gave Dec before he left. Dec lost his during his attack."

Okay. I wasn't aware he had his military cell on him, but I guess he had to just in case.

Leaving him on the sidewalk, Mac and I made our way to the café and headed inside to find a table.

"He'll catch up," she answered to my silent question of wondering if Dec would know we'd gone on ahead.

"Do you think they'll send Dec overseas too?" I asked, looking around the busy café and sniffing in delightful aromas of coffee and fresh food.

Vegetarianism must be thriving, judging by the patronage and fast-paced atmosphere. We sat at the only vacant table with four seats at the back. Dec still hadn't arrived, so Mac and I picked up a menu, ready to order.

My friend didn't look too concerned at my question. "He's got a twelve-month reprieve due to his recovering gunshot wound and mental state after the amnesia, abduction, and memory return. He's safe for a while yet."

"Will it bother you if he gets called away down

the track when he's fit for duty again?" She hadn't experienced her man off to war yet. She'd only witnessed first-hand the effects it had on her soldier. I imagine she'd be just as worried as I was about Viper fighting for his life and country. Who wouldn't be? And I wasn't even Viper's girlfriend.

Breathing out hard and pinning me with an intense stare, she answered, "I hate the thought, to be honest. I don't want him to return to duty, but I know I can't ask him to leave, either. It's his life. I'll be a mess the whole time he's away. It's a case of when, not if."

"I understand you'd never ask him to give it up, but hypothetically speaking, do you think he would if you did ask?"

Leaving my gaze for the menu on the table, she turned it over, stalling. "I'm not sure. Part of me would like to think so, but deep down I get how important it is to defend his country. It's a part of him."

She appeared troubled by it, so I changed the subject. "Do you think we should wait to order? For Dec?" I asked.

"Nah. I'm starved. He won't mind if we start."

I didn't want to think of the future when she'd lose her man to another mission. I struggled with the 'no contact' rule every day. I just needed to know Viper remained safe.

A waitress came over and took our orders. I decided on a pumpkin salad, and Mac ordered a chick-pea burger with a healthy vegetable juice for each of us.

The waitress had just taken our menus and was

walking to the kitchen when Dec appeared. His face had drawn in, his eyes dark and dangerous. His entire energy had shifted from relaxed to extremely tense. Mac sat up straight, noticing too.

"Hey. Everything okay?"

Dec sat down heavily opposite me and something in my psyche cracked. My heart upped its tempo as blood surged. The earlier sensation of anxiety escalated.

His jaw held firm as he ground out. "Viper's been injured. Stepped on a land-mine." He dropped his head, and I couldn't tell if he was crying or not. My stomach left me and my lungs expanded on a loud gasp.

"What? Is he all right? When did this happen?" I felt sick.

Mac had a hand to her throat, her eyes wide and fearful. Her other hand went to Dec's shoulder.

When his head lifted, pain mapped his features. "He's being flown to Germany from Iraq. His leg…"

The room spun. Sounds evaporated, except for Dec's voice and all of our breathing. My fears had been confirmed. The odd sensation I couldn't pinpoint. Had it been a forewarning?

Shit. No. I had to be dreaming.

"His leg?" Mac spoke when I couldn't.

"It took a lot of the blast."

A whimper escaped. Nausea lifted to my throat and I had to swallow thickly to avoid throwing up. Tears welled in my eyes at the horror of what Viper had gone through. Was still going through.

The only thing I could think of to ask was, "Why

Germany?"

It sounded dumb.

"The nature of the injury. A lot of troops get sent to Germany if they have extensive trauma."

Fuck! I didn't swear often but my head was full of *fucks*.

"Do you want to head home?" Mac asked, attempting to be the strong one. God bless her.

Fisting his hair, Dec shrugged. "I don't know what the hell to do. My best buddy is on route to fricking Germany and here I sit, in a café in Ann Arbor, and there isn't a thing I can do to help him or comfort him." His fists clenched and unclenched, leaving his dark strands a mess.

Not hungry now, I agreed.

"Let's get our food to go and head home."

Mac nodded. "I'll go and let the waitress know to pack it up."

How things could change in an instant! I remembered Viper jogging at a preposterous hour of the morning on my way home from work. His strong, toned legs had carried him forward with ease. Now…perhaps he'd never run again. Never serve again. The military would pension him off. He'd have to start over.

A million thoughts vied for a space in my head. Vaguely I heard Mac motioning me up, before gripping my arm and leading me out, after handing Dec a large white bag with our food.

The drive home passed in a sea of visions. Imagining what Viper had gone through. The pain. Had he been alone? Had he been conscious? How long had he lain injured? What ran through his mind?

"Pull over!" I yelled, feeling the bile rise.

Dec turned sideways attempting to look at me in the backseat. "What? Why?"

Mac looked at me and must have seen the look on my face. "Pull over. Now."

The car swerved and came to a stop along the gutter of a street not far away from the apartment.

Thrusting the door open, I barely made it out when I retched. Doors opened and closed. Acid lodged in my throat as my stomach turned over again. A warm hand landed on my back, rubbing.

"Char? You okay?"

Why did people always ask that? Blind Freddy could see I was far from fine. Retching again, I willed my stomach to settle while taking deep breaths. The cool air helped.

My brain couldn't shut off images of Viper being blown up. The more the movie played on continuous loop, the more nauseous I became, until the contents of my stomach abruptly let fly all over the freshly mowed grass outside a modest suburban house.

My hair lifted out of my face courtesy of one of my friends. I couldn't tell who it was because my head stayed downcast, my hips bent forward.

"It's okay. Just take a moment and keep breathing," Mac soothed. "I have some antacid tablets in my bag. I'll get them."

She moved away, leaving me with Dec, who I quickly found out was the one holding my hair. It made me love him that little bit more.

"Thank you," I offered, the deep, prolonged

breathing finally beginning to take effect.

"Sure. I guess the news of Viper's accident has hit a nerve, huh?"

I didn't answer. Of course it had hit a nerve. Who wouldn't be upset over the news of someone they knew? I didn't want to explain just how much the news had hit me.

Mac touched my arm. "Here. Chew this tablet. It should help settle the acid back down."

I took the chalky pill and stuck it under my tongue, disliking the taste.

"I'm sorry. I don't know what came over me." Lie. I knew damn well.

Standing fully, I waited for the dizziness to fade and began shuffling to the car. I didn't miss the look between Mac and Dec. As if they knew exactly why I'd become sick. They weren't stupid.

I just wanted to get back to the apartment, take a shower, go to bed, and wake up to discover it had all been a bad dream. Wishful thinking.

Chapter Eighteen

Viper

Heat. Desert dust. Rigged to kill. I was in my element. After a successful brief, and a long flight, I arrived at our base, or rather our shanty of tents hidden in the belly of the surrounding Afghan mountains. Even under the canopy of night, a hive of activity surrounded me and the fifteen other soldiers who'd been brought in to assist with a ground attack on a rebel group who were trying to take a town over the other side of the ranges. We had a two-hour hike ahead of us. Brutal conditions existed in this part of the world. Only the tough survived. We were the toughest. Two tanks were preparing to assist with the takeover. I preferred to be on foot. To feel the earth underneath. Instead of having armored steel around me, my inner warrior preferred the thrill and risk of being a target. Most men in my unit felt the same. The fear of not knowing one second from the next if a bullet or bomb would take you out.

Sick, I knew, but that was me.

I'd slept a good portion of the flight, knowing it would probably be the most I'd get for a while. In between waking and dozing, thoughts had switched to Char. I wondered what she was doing. Had she settled in at Mac's? I shouldn't have been letting my mind wander, but I couldn't help it. Leaving her had been harder than I imagined. A piece of my heart had been left back in Ann Arbor and I wasn't sure how to process it.

I was a world away from the comfort of her arms, yet I could still smell her perfume, mixed in with the smell of sweat, artillery, and the constant threats of war.

"Soldier! You with me?" barked my commanding officer.

"Yes, sir!" I responded.

He glared at me under the spotlight that lit up the sergeant's tent, attempting to believe my half-truth. No. I couldn't let Red ruin this for me. I needed full focus. Sucking in a couple of deep breaths, I settled. My hand came up to clasp my dog tags, grounding me again. Char was safe at home where she belonged. I had a job to do, and I needed to do it efficiently.

Leaning into me, my boss whispered in my ear, "You can't handle the heat, go home."

It was that simple. I wouldn't let him or my team down.

Pushing all thoughts of Char away, I nodded. "I'm fine, sir!"

"Make sure you are."

Leaning away and moving down the line of

soldiers standing at attention, he yelled, "Anyone else need to run home to Mommy?"

Not one person moved an inch. We all wanted to be there. We all had the same separation anxiety issues.

Once Sarge seemed satisfied we were all in compliance, he proceeded to inform us of our mission.

"We attack from the east. Take out the entire cell. No prisoners. I repeat. No prisoners. It's going to take some time. Weeks. I suggest you get comfortable in your new home, boys. We head out in approximately," he glanced at his watch, "one hour and forty minutes. Dismissed."

We saluted our leader and filed away to our digs. I shared with three other guys, two of them I'd worked with before.

***

Same situation as other times. We trudged on foot to our destination. Night goggles on. The clock had read one a.m. when we'd left camp. Rigged up to the hilt. Fifteen soldiers. Men with lives back home. Parents. Wives. Partners. Children. To look at them now though, none of that existed. Only the battle ahead. The realness of the moment. Nothing registering but every tiny sound. Every movement. Our weighted gear keeping us grounded.

In another ten minutes, we'd be in enemy territory. The surrounding terrain held no life. Sparse. Rocky. The ridge up ahead would lead us to a very dim view of the village, overtaken by rebels who had no idea we were almost upon them. With a partial moon, we had to rely on our source, who'd infiltrated the town weeks earlier. He was our eyes and ears. We wanted to strike at night with the element of surprise. Hopeful that most of the rebels would be asleep, we'd take out the ones left to keep guard.

The starlit sky kept us company as we neared our lookout. We kept hydrated while the sweat continued to flow. While we were all extremely fit and trained for these conditions, my legs ached. An ache I had long ago learned to ignore. Push past the pain. It was all mental from here on out.

Our leader motioned us up the hill to the peak where we would all rest and assess the situation below.

Some of our fifteen may not walk out alive, myself included. I could only trust my judgment and instincts and skill as a soldier to save my life. But we all had the attitude that if we died saving our country and others, then our sacrifice would be worth it.

Unloading our gear for a short reprieve and to regroup, we crouched low, assessing our target town. It was hard to gauge the view of the town in the darkened bosom of the rocky hillside. I could see, however, how far the buildings spread. It was bigger than I imagined, the crumbling shapes filling in an otherwise dusty, flat expanse.

"Okay. Listen up. Our guy has spotted eight armed men surrounding the town. Two at north, east, south, and west. We'll split up into five groups of three. Once we've disabled the immediate threat, we'll regroup."

"Viper, Lazerus, and McVeigh you're on the east side. Dodge, Maverick, and Thompson, take care of the south…"

I didn't hear the rest. It only mattered who I was teamed up with. I hadn't worked with Lazerus or McVeigh, before so I hoped they had their game on. We didn't need any cock-ups whatsoever or death would come quick. Apparently, they had good reputations, but it would remain to be seen as far as I was concerned.

We rested for a few minutes, then it was go time. We fanned out into our groups, and with a signal from Sarge, we crested the rise.

Weapons raised and ready to fire, we slid down the other side and stealthily crept into town. I held front position while Lazerus and McVeigh flanked me.

The others had moved to their coordinates, leaving the three of us open targets.

The beauty of entering such a rundown, uncivilized settlement proved to be a blessing. It sat mainly in darkness, save for a few scattered lights, dimly shining.

Moving across the perimeter to the east side, we stopped at the furthest building. I motioned to my guys to stay put while I checked around the corner for the enemy. It couldn't be so easy, surely.

My soldier mind had me conjuring up all kinds of scenarios. One being that we were entering a trap. Had our insider given us the correct information? Trust wasn't something that came easily to me. Especially after the no-show of backup during Dec's rescue.

Taking a step around the corner, scanning everywhere for heat in my thermal goggles, I took pause. Finding nothing, I urged Lazerus and McVeigh on with me. My heart thundered a glorious tune in my chest. Adrenalin, at an all-time high, gave me the power to do what I needed to.

We moved like sleek panthers, slow and steady. The ground broke away in parts, a messy cluster of upended earth, posing as a road. A noise sounded akin to metal scraping. We flattened ourselves against a stone wall, my breath ceasing in order to hear better.

A flare of unease crept up my body. I didn't like the feeling, but in order to do my job properly, I pushed it aside. After waiting and hearing nothing more, we continued on. Dated vehicles sat haphazardly outside mud-brick dwellings, zigzagged together in no particular order, with taller ones dwarfing the smaller ones.

A shape appeared in my goggles up ahead. It exited a house. The guy was armed and staring up the road with his back to us. I nodded to Lazerus, who crouched and moved from behind the vehicle, taking aim and firing. The guy dropped instantly. We waited for repercussions, expecting retaliation, but all was silent again. With the collapsed enemy ahead, we assumed there was only one other threat left on our side, so we stood and moved forward, fingers on our triggers.

Inching toward the fallen, I noticed the clean shot right through his head. He'd had no chance. Lazerus had skill but then again he wouldn't be operating with the elite if he didn't.

Impressed, I gave him my best nod with my headgear in place.

Movement up ahead made my head pivot forward, placing my finger up to warn my guys.

Out of an alley to the left, movement again, and a shot rang out. It missed us, but hit the mud brick wall next to us, sending bits of the dried earth flying apart.

I motioned for Lazerus and McVeigh to fan out as we crossed the road. Silly move on the shooters behalf if the alley had a dead end. My finger was itching to press the trigger. I could almost feel a twitch, but I held it steady. Heat came into my view as we approached. Without a second thought, the three of us fired, sending the target to the dirt. Two down. Easy enough. But like before, unease slithered back into my chest. Spinning in all directions, I cleared the short passageway before moving out.

If anyone in the town worried about the gunfire, they didn't stir to find out. They were probably used to it after having rebels take over, killing and maiming at random.

I wondered how the others were doing.

We needed to meet up now that our targets had been taken down. Sending a quick text on my military radio, I asked for our point of contact.

In a flash, I had a reply. Western side. Abandoned building. Freestanding, just out of town. Coordinates given. So far everything had gone smoothly. Why then did the niggling feeling of doom continue to plague me?

Rounding the bend, we apprehensively walked toward our coordinates, aiming at anything that moved. Residents remained indoors. Smart on their behalf, because the way I felt, they'd most likely suffer a bullet to the head. Firing off some rounds had fed the sick monster inside. The feel of the powerful rifle under my fingers. Hearing the sound of the bullet leaving the barrel. Watching the enemy drop. It all fueled the desire for mortal combat.

Beginning the climb away from the hub of buildings, my group spanned out into a pyramid shape, remaining on high alert. Never let the guard down. Just because we were away from trouble didn't mean we were out of danger.

Our boots hit the rocky terrain again as the rise we'd taken peaked and then descended, leaving the town behind us, hidden once again. A sigh left me at that point. Glad to be away from it, but knowing our mission had only begun, I'd be glad to finish the day and get a shower and some shut-eye later. I wasn't sure what awaited us once we regrouped, but we would soon find out. We were on point with our coordinates, the sun beginning to drag itself up over the horizon.

The meeting point hadn't emerged into view, but I knew we still had a way to go.

Before I could place one foot in front of the other to take my next step, a loud blast sounded the split second before I became airborne, thrown backward in an explosion of rock and dust. I didn't know what hit me before losing consciousness.

***

Coming around, faces faded in and out. Voices and pieces of words a jumble. My vision wavered, spots dangling and dancing in front of my eyes.

"Viper…hold on…don't move…we're getting you out of here." Screaming. Lots of screaming. Numbness. I was on my back unable to move. What the hell happened?

Curses flew. Not from me, but from those shrouding me. I needed to sleep. My body melded into the ground as if it wanted to become a part of it.

Closing my eyes against the shapes and colors, the last thing I heard and felt was someone's large hand slapping my face, yelling, "Don't go to sleep, man. Stay awake."

Too late.

At odd intervals, I woke and then slept. Movement had me attempt to open my eyes, but the action proved too hard.

My body, a heavy weight, sank into whatever I lay on until I was out to it again.

In the darkness, I swam. Looking for something. Anything to anchor me. I felt nothing. Saw nothing. If death had stolen me, was this it? Was this what happened to us all? And yet my conscious mind remained. Aware of the black. Aware of the awareness. Or perhaps I'd landed in hell. Destined to spend eternity cognizant of nothing but my own thoughts.

I wanted to laugh at the irony of that notion, but couldn't manage it without a voice. I was nothing—and yet I remained *something*.

Time ceased to exist and so I remained suspended in an alternate universe. Flashes of memory bled into the dark space. Faces. War. Guns. Battle. A woman. Oh yes. A woman. Fiery red hair and eyes like the forest. She stood out from all the other muck, blocking out the encompassing void for a moment as I grasped onto the hallucination. Like a ray of warm light piercing through gloomy gray clouds, I needed it. Needed…her.

Hell turned into Heaven as I immersed myself in her image. The laughter in her eyes giving me a sense of peace. A sense of belonging. An epiphany cleared some of the fog. Yes. That's it. She was home. My home.

Chapter Nineteen

Char

Once home, I stood under the burning shower spray to help alleviate the tension wracking my body. Right down to my bones I could feel it. Sorrow. Pain. Worry. As a nurse I'd seen some pretty horrific injuries, but not to someone I knew and cared about. Yes, cared about. I could admit it now. I did care. More than I should, but Viper was different. He challenged me in every way. Maybe that's why I'd always kept men at a distance and opted for casual. It had been the excuse for my long working hours. I needed someone strong who upended my world and made me work for what I wanted. Someone to keep me on my toes. Most men I'd dated, doctors included, bored me to tears. It was always the same mundane conversations about the weather, my job. Small talk. I needed more. Deep within me, I'd always known, but it had taken a stubborn, arrogant soldier to find and unlock the dormant key to my needs.

Damn. I think I'd just had the revelation of all revelations.

Whatever the extent of Viper's injuries, I needed to be there for him no matter what. He only had Dec and Mac. He'd helped me in my time of weakness. I'd do the same. I was no psychologist, but I'd had to counsel plenty of patients through trauma while under my care.

Who knew what mindset Viper would be in? How would he react to the likelihood of not being able to return to combat? Ever. That alone may destroy him.

Scrubbing myself and drying off, I settled into my pajamas and walked into the living room to find Mac and Dec huddled together talking quietly. Glancing up at the sound of my approach, they both gave me pitiful smiles.

"Any word?" I asked, eying the food we'd taken from the restaurant on the coffee table.

Nabbing mine, not hungry but knowing I needed sustenance of some kind, I sat and unwrapped the parcel, feeling two sets of eyes on me.

"How are you feeling now?" Mac queried softly.

Numb, but I wasn't about to say that. "Okay. Shocked. Saddened." Swinging my gaze to Dec, I asked, "Have you heard anything more?"

Shaking his head, he answered, "No, but I'll keep pushing for answers."

My selfishness and own emotions had stopped me from thinking about Dec. His best friend had been struck by a landmine. He knew only what we knew. I could only imagine how he felt.

Reaching out across Mac, I touched his arm.

"I'm sorry. You must be gutted too. You've known him a lot longer than we have." My eyes flew between Mac and I.

Clearing his throat and then rubbing his face, he said, "Of all the things that could go wrong in battle, I never imagined a mine getting him." He stood, kissing Mac on the head. I could tell he was barely keeping it together. "I'm gonna head out for a bit. Sitting here waiting on the phone to ring is doing my head in."

Mac stood and put her arms around him. "I'm so sorry you have to go through this worry. He's such a strong guy. He'll pull through."

"I know. It's not his survival I'm stressed about. It's the after-effects and recovery."

He had the same mindset as me, knowing full well his friend would mentally be a mess after this. He already wore the internal and external scars of a soldier. If he was left maimed in any way that hindered his ability to continue to fight for his country, it could prove detrimental.

After Dec drove off in his truck, Mac and I sat quietly, neither of us knowing what to say. She remained in her head and I remained in mine, going over and over Viper's accident.

Overcome with fatigue, I stood. "I'm going to take a nap. Are you okay?"

Smiling up at me, she nodded. "Yeah. You go. I'll be fine. I'm going to bake some cookies to help take my mind off it."

I thought that was odd. I'd never seen my friend bake cookies. Perhaps it was her way of dealing.

Once in my room, I stretched out on the bed,

letting sleep pull me under.

It was dark when I awoke. Sounds of raised voices seeped through the walls. For a second, disorientation had me sit up and rub at my eyes, but remembering the news from earlier, I groaned and rose, wanting to know what the commotion was.

Opening the bedroom door, I stopped, wondering if I should let them hash it out. I caught some of the conversation and decided I needed to support my friend, who appeared distressed.

"Calm down, honey. It's okay. You've been drinking…"

"Calm the fuck down? How am I supposed to calm the fuck down? My brother is in God knows what state, and I'm sitting over here on my ass waiting for someone to tell me more." I heard something break and upped my pace down the hallway, only to discover Mac pressed up against the counter while Dec stood in a rage on the opposite side, glass splattered everywhere as if he'd thrown it at the wall.

Both of them spun and stared at me as I neared.

"Ah, what's going on?"

I looked at Mac. Her face was pinched, eyes dripping with tears. Instantly I was at her side, my arm across her shoulder.

I could smell alcohol fumes across the kitchen. Dec wavered on his feet, eyes bloodshot, fists clenched.

The situation needed to be diffused quickly.

"Dec, let's go sit in the living room and talk. Do you want a coffee?" I offered, attempting to keep my voice calm.

Eyeing me, he barked, "You think that's going to help?" Clutching at his hair, desperate, he yelled, "I should have been there! I should have protected him!"

So that's what bothered him? He felt torn because he hadn't been with Viper on the mission. He thought his presence may have averted the disaster.

"You couldn't possibly have done that." As soon as the words left my mouth, I knew I shouldn't have said them. I heard Mac's sharp inhale.

Dec's eyes blazed. He strode over to us. I knew he wouldn't do anything to hurt us, but he was no less intimidating. "How can you say that? You have no idea. I've always had his back and he's always had mine."

I wanted to yell back that invisible mines under the ground could go off at any time and no amount of protection could avoid them detonating when they were ready. But I held back.

Instead, I appeased him. "You're right. I can understand how you feel. I'd feel the same if it were Mac." Squeezing her shoulder, I kept my focus on the towering wall of anger in front of us. "So let's think. How can we get the information you need without you physically having to travel to Germany?"

I didn't have the answers. I was merely trying to calm him down. His eyes twinkled and I could tell the cogs of his brain were turning. As if flicking a switch, his entire demeanor changed. Gripping me by the shoulders he planted a solid kiss on my head. "I fucking knew we had you around for a reason.

Char, you're a genius!"
 Mac piped up, "What do you mean?"
 "I'm going to Germany!"

Chapter Twenty

Viper

My eyes opened and fought against the bright light. Squeezing them shut and then re-opening them, my vision focused on a room. The last I remembered I'd been walking with my team to safety after taking out our targets.

Attempting to sit up, I found it impossible. My body was numb from the waist down. A brown-haired twenty-something nurse hovered close by. It was obvious I had landed in the hospital.

Upon my awakening, she smiled. "Welcome back." She spoke in broken English. Her pale skin and blue eyes were the exact opposite of most Afghan women I'd met. Was she working in an Arabian hospital? Maybe she'd been posted here.

Wires and tubes came out of my body beneath the blankets which covered me. A heart monitor beeped monotonously. Outside the window, grey skies lingered above more of the concrete structure I lay in.

"Surgery went well," she said, moving to my bed to check the IV line hooked up to a bag of fluid.

"Surgery?"

How badly had I been injured? Did I suffer a bullet wound? I'd survived others, but this felt different.

"Yes. The surgeons managed to save three-quarters of your leg."

What. The. Actual. Fuck? My leg?

Panic seized me as I grappled with the sheets to peer below. I could only move from the waist up. Her words slaughtered me as my eyes zeroed in on my bandaged leg. Crap. Crap. My heart stopped for a moment as I gaped at the shorter limb. A bandaged stump finishing where my knee should have been.

A sound leached from my throat. A whimper mixed with a fierce growl.

The worried nurse still stood beside me, placing her hand on my shoulder in a show of comfort, but it did little to stop the insane reality from squeezing all the air from my lungs.

"I lost my leg? How?"

"You were lucky you didn't lose it all. You stepped on a landmine."

My brain tried to remember. Nothing gelled. Shock embraced me. I couldn't piece together anything.

I realized I could have been killed, but to lose a limb? To be deformed? It would change my world. My job. In the space of a second, I'd become disabled. Flashes of being pensioned off like a leper, lost and forgotten, stole my focus. I didn't hear what the nurse said, only her voice, faint and muffled as if under water.

I'd lost part of my leg. My toes. My foot. I'd never walk again, unless under the steam of a prosthetic. Shit. How do I deal with that?

A doctor entered. He too appeared of European descent. Confusion made me ask, "Where am I?"

"You were flown to Germany overnight. You're in Landstuhl Regional Medical Center."

My head swam. "Germany?" I knew soldiers were brought here for surgery, but to not be aware of the flight and to wake up in another country was very alarming.

"How long will I be here?"

"Until you've stabilized. Then a military officer will fly you home."

Home. It would forever be altered. I'd forever be altered.

"I'll be back in a little while to check on you. How are your pain levels?"

"I can't feel anything below the waist." Why couldn't I feel my right leg? Thank fuck my left leg had taken the explosion.

"That's a good thing. You're numb from surgery. The anesthetic and epidural will wear off in a little while."

Epidural? I thought only women in labor received those.

Closing my eyes to my new reality, I let the doctor and nurse pad out. I couldn't even turn over because of the numbness, so I lay on my back, staring at the ceiling, trying to let everything sink in and settle.

As I tried to do this, a vision of a stunning redhead swamped me. Striking eyes.

Body made for sin. A fire in her soul rivaling Hades. For a moment, I let the memory of her draw me in before reality kicked in.

I'd never be able to give her what she needed now. The one woman I could see myself falling for could never love me. I couldn't bear to see the pity in those glorious eyes. The sadness. She didn't deserve to be encumbered with a lesser man. She deserved a partner who could give her the world, not just pieces.

I fought the onset of tears. I'd only ever cried at my parents' funerals. Funny now, how knowing I'd never have Red the way I wanted her, felt like the same loss all over again.

I always assumed war would take my life. I'd die doing what I loved. I never imagined it would dangle death in front of me and torment me into wishing I no longer breathed. No longer having to go through the motions of being half a person. To leave me questioning my existence.

Loneliness stabbed me all over, twisting my organs this way and that. Never before had the world seemed like it was about to swallow me whole.

Chapter Twenty-One

Char

Mac and I had attempted to talk Dec out of his hair-brained idea of traveling to Germany, but he wouldn't have any of it. In the end, I'd agreed to go with him for company as Mac had used all her work leave and I still had four weeks up my sleeve. After much deliberation, it had been settled. Work had been notified and here I currently sat, in the International Departure lounge at Detroit Metropolitan Airport waiting for our fifteen-hour flight to be called. We'd have two stops along the way. I hoped to sleep for some of it because I hadn't done much since hearing of Viper's accident.

Dec sat beside me on the hard chairs, his foot jerking up and down nervously.

"You worried about what you'll find when we get there?" I asked.

Staying focused on the screen of his cell, he sighed. "Sure, but regardless, I'm not going to let on to Viper. He needs my full support. I'm trying to mentally prepare myself."

A female voice announced a different flight, so I waited to respond. "At least I'm practiced in the art of remaining stony-faced," I joked, but he didn't laugh. I couldn't blame him. As much as he would never admit it, I knew he agonized over his friend. The hows and whys of it all. The what ifs. Viper was lucky to have Dec, and vice-versa. I'd never met two grown men who were so loyal. They truly were family in every sense of the word, except blood. They had a lifelong bond forged through battle and it could never be broken.

We waited another half hour before our flight was called, fifteen minutes late.

Finding our seats toward the back of the plane, I was grateful Dec offered me the window seat. Such a long flight called for some sort of view into the outside world. The longest I'd ever flown had been years earlier to Los Angeles to visit my cousin.

We got settled, and before long we were cruising at thirty-two thousand feet. I asked the one question plaguing me. "Do you think he'll be pleased to see us?"

"I hope so. I'm the only family he has. It's gotta be lonely for him without a support network."

Would he be happy to see me though? It's not like he'd left on bad terms, but would he want me seeing him in whatever state he was in?

"How long do you think they'll keep him in Germany?" I asked, wondering if he'd even still be there when we arrived.

"Depends on the extent of his injuries. A week, maybe."

Let's hope that information proved correct or the entire trip would be a waste of time and money.

We'd paid way more than we should for the tickets because we needed to fly urgently, but I guess that's a small price for getting to Viper.

I recalled the hot night we'd shared. For a few hours, I'd felt connected to him. I felt like he actually cared. Maybe sex would be the extent of his ability to show affection to a woman. Maybe he carried too many demons inside to give himself over to another totally. But what about the woman he'd been engaged to? Surely she'd had his complete heart, otherwise, why commit yourself to a lifetime with someone?

My thoughts were interrupted by a steward offering drinks. Dec accepted a beer and I opted for a can of Coke. Alcohol wasn't on my agenda at the moment. I couldn't think of anything other than getting to Viper and making sure he would be okay.

The flight became tedious. I slept on and off, as did Dec, in between watching movies.

We didn't share conversation much, other than necessary small talk, which suited me fine. I was all in my own head and didn't have it in me to carry on with idle chatter. Glad that Dec felt the same, I closed my eyes and willed the flight to be over.

***

When we finally touched down on German soil, I felt disoriented and fatigued. We were in a different time zone and a country which spoke another language.

After collecting our bags, we made our way to a cab so we could travel the thirty minutes to Landstuhl, where the military hospital was located.

Dec had booked accommodation there so we would be close to Viper.

Luckily the cab driver spoke some English, so we were able to communicate with him about our destination.

My nerves ratcheted up a notch, leaving me with a sour taste in my mouth and swirling nausea in my gut. Dec had more sleep than me, but still, he appeared as if he'd had none. The stress of why we'd traveled to Germany began to really hit home.

What would we find? Would Viper be so disfigured we wouldn't recognize him? Had his handsome face been marred? With each mile closer, I felt like I wanted to throw up.

Dec's whole body fidgeted. I don't even think he realized he did it.

"How much further?" he asked the driver.

"About another ten miles," he replied in broken English.

God. It felt like we'd been traveling for days.

Dec had called Mac to let her know we'd arrived safely and that we'd update her when we found out Viper's condition.

I desperately needed a hot shower. None of this seemed real. I felt out of my body, looking in from afar. I stared out the window but saw nothing.

"How you holding up?" Dec broke through my mundane staring.

"Nervous. You?"

"Glad to be getting closer. I just want to see

him."

I did, but I didn't. I needed to see with my own eyes that he was alive, but on the other side of the coin, I wasn't ready for the sight awaiting me. Was I overreacting? Were his injuries going to be less than what I pictured? I didn't normally anticipate the worst, but for some reason, the idea of surviving a landmine had my brain conjuring up some macabre images I couldn't shake.

"Char?"

"Hmm?"

"I'm glad you're here." He squeezed my arm and attempted a smile, but it twisted at one side.

"Me too."

We booked into our less than stellar hotel and each took a shower and got cleaned up before heading out again. We were both eager to see Viper for our own reasons and couldn't delay it any longer.

It was morning in Germany, so visiting hours would be open. I'd changed into some casual jeans with a long-sleeved top and a leather jacket. The temperature was cool and the skies remained overcast.

The military hospital looked unassuming. A two-story concrete structure spread out with a large sign reading Landstuhl Regional Medical Center. Another sign read 'Emergency Room.' The cab driver dropped us outside the Emergency Department.

Staff in military uniforms entered and exited the premises.

"We need to find the regular entrance. A & E

will just send us there anyway."

Agreeing that Viper would have been transferred to a ward by now, we walked under a large canopy and into the organized chaos.

Spotting the main reception area, we approached a nurse. "Excuse me?"

"Yes. How can I help?"

"We're here to see Charlie O'Dowell. He's been here a few days."

She eyed us both. "Are you family?"

Glancing my way, and then back to the woman, Dec spoke. "He doesn't have a family. I'm all he has. I've flown all the way from the States to see him."

I couldn't begin to imagine how Dec would respond if we were turned away.

The middle-aged nurse turned to her computer and typed in some things before regarding Declan.

"Room sixty-three. Follow the hallway, turn right, and you'll see signs with room numbers for different wings of the center."

Nodding, Dec grabbed my arm and pulled me away, not waiting another second.

The hospital bustled with medical staff and military personnel. The familiar smell of disinfectant washed over me and I almost felt at home as we followed the long corridor before turning as the nurse instructed. Finding numbers 25–65, we kept up our hurried pace until room 63 appeared. Dec still had a hold of my arm. I don't think he realized he still held it. I could tell every muscle in him had tightened. I steeled myself for what awaited us beyond that door. We still didn't know the extent of Viper's injuries and had to be ready for the worst.

I attempted to go into nurse mode, but it was hard knowing the victim.

"Are you ready?" I quietly asked Dec.

His breath had deepened as he eyed me, glancing down to where he held me. He let go, cracking his neck.

"Ready as I'll ever be."

Pushing open the door, I nearly stumbled when I caught sight of Viper.

Chapter Twenty-Two

Viper

I'd dozed on and off, frustrated at not being able to move. Supposedly I was getting out of bed at some stage today. That would be fun. I didn't want some damn wheelchair. I wanted crutches. The idea of being in a wheelchair turned my stomach. I didn't want to be some pitiful charity case getting stared at while trying to push my way through crowds or unable to enter restaurants and buildings that didn't cater to disabled people.

My room door opened, stealing my thoughts and my breath. I had to be dreaming. It couldn't be.

Two people a world away from mine right now ambled into my room as if I wasn't lying in a Goddamn hospital bed with half my leg blown away. What the—?

My face must have shown shock because Dec proceeded to grin like an asshole while I gave him only a couple of seconds of my time before focusing on a pair of stunning green eyes. Eyes I'd been dreaming of. Eyes I'd been beating myself up over because they'd never see me the same again.

She smiled. It seemed genuine enough, but still, I couldn't bring myself to close my gaping mouth to speak.

"Hey, shit for brains. If you wanted to get out of your mission, you could have done it differently."

Hearing his voice choked me up. I looked back at him. My brother. The only person I had in this lonely world. He'd flown halfway around the globe to be here for me. He never let me down. His loyalty was unwavering.

When he neared, I nearly lost my shit, unable to swallow past the emotion lodged in my chest and throat.

He held out his hand and I stared at it for a moment as if it wasn't really there. This wasn't really happening.

"You gonna ignore me or what?" he badgered, still with that damn grin spreading his cheeks.

Lifting my arm, I gripped his hand like a lifeline. I squeezed. He squeezed harder. Before I knew it, he'd leaned down and was giving me the closest thing to a hug he could while I remained lying down.

"I love you, man." He said it so only I could hear and a tear escaped my left eye. One solo drip cascading down my cheek. A strange noise left me as I nodded, attempting to pull myself together.

I didn't do emotional bullshit with Dec. We laughed and badgered each other but this…this was foreign. I didn't know how to respond.

The room remained silent until I heard the

shuffling of delicate feet.

Dec stood and we both watched Char ease closer.

I hadn't said a word to her. She chewed the inside of her mouth nervously. A sense of déjà vu hit me.

Not too long ago, I'd been in Dec's position while he lay in a hospital bed. Mac had visited him, and due to his PTSD, he'd turned her away, unable to cope with seeing her. I'd called him out for being a dick and here I lay, wanting to do the same thing. I knew exactly how he felt. He'd wanted her gone to protect her. From him.

I wanted more than anything to tell her to go. To get as far away from me as possible. To move on. The only problem was that while staring her down and seeing her compassionate expression, I couldn't do it. Not now, anyway. She'd come so far with Dec. It would be an asshole thing to do.

Instead, I offered her a, "Hi."

Her cheek popped out as her teeth stopped chewing it and she walked to stand beside Dec.

"Hi. You look…good."

Good? Right. Who was she kidding? I knew I had marks on my face from shrapnel. If she looked underneath my bedding, she'd know I was far from fine. How much had they been told? Did they know the extent of my injuries?

"Don't lie, Red. I look like shit. You don't have to be nice."

"Nah, man, it's true. We didn't know what to expect. Couldn't get info from anyone. They said your leg took a lot of the blast. Better that than your face disfigured, right? Once your leg heals, you'll be good as new."

Shit. They didn't have a clue.

Before₁ I could answer, the door opened again and a nurse with a trolley strolled in.

"Oh good, you're awake." She glanced at my visitors. "I'm here to change your dressing. If your visitors are squeamish, I advise them to wait outside."

Keeping my eyes focused on my friends, I watched them exchange a glance. Probably silently exchanging the nurse's words to each other.

"I'm a nurse." Char smiled. "There's nothing I can't handle."

Dec nodded with her. They weren't leaving.

They also didn't know just what they were about to witness as the nurse moved to the side of my bed and proceeded to pull down the blankets.

I wanted to look away. I didn't want to see their reactions, but it was like watching a horror movie. I just had to keep watching regardless.

Two sets of eyes widened at the sight of half my leg missing. Red let out a gasp as she grabbed her throat. Dec tightened and let loose a curse.

I felt vulnerable. Exposed.

The nurse gave them one last chance. "You sure you want to stay for this?"

Donning a pair of gloves, she took pause, garnering their response.

Red's head pivoted up to mine. And there it was. The pity I so desperately didn't want. She couldn't hide it no matter how brave she tried to be. I witnessed other emotions flit across her face too, and I knew at that moment everything had changed for us. Between us. The weight of my injury became a heavy burden. I could almost see her mind ticking over as a million thoughts took hold in her brain. Her bottom lip quivered. I didn't want her tears any more than I wanted her pity. It all happened in a couple of seconds. She shook her head, glancing away from me. "I'm staying."

"Me too," said Dec.

I knew they were only trying to be strong for me. After they left, they'd probably fall apart and voice their true feelings.

Like the good soldier he was, Dec stepped forward, schooling his features again. He placed a hand on my shoulder. "We're in this together. I got you. I'm here as long as you need."

He knew me well. He knew not to utter the words, "I'm so sorry." No matter how much he wanted to say them. For that I was grateful. Red, however, stood stock still, not quite knowing how to act. She fervently watched the nurse changing the dressing, her eyes darting to mine every so often.

"Thanks, man." The lump I'd had lodged in my throat from earlier released and a world of pent-up sensations exploded in my chest. No amount of trying to tamp it down could stop it from erupting. A sob escaped, flaying me open further than I already was. With my raw wound bared to the two people who meant more to me than anyone else, they could see the true me. The me I didn't let anyone else see. My eyes clouded over from tears and my face screwed up in anguish.

The deep, racking howls caught everyone by surprise, even me.

The nurse gave me her attention. "Can I get you anything?" She was almost finished and I just wanted her gone.

"No," I spluttered out, wiping my eyes with the back of my hand. Dec's hand squeezed my shoulder but he remained quiet, letting me grieve.

I didn't need words. I needed my fucking leg back. My life. The only life I knew.

Losing a part of you, no matter how big or small, brought with it a certain amount of grief. I'd never have that part of me back. Ever.

The nurse graciously left, leaving tension in her wake. I stared out the window at nothing in particular, leaving my friends to deal with my meltdown themselves.

My sobbing eased and only emptiness remained.

My body and soul were tired. I didn't think I could live with my disability. To change my whole way of existing. Why hadn't the bomb taken me completely?

"Viper?"

My head turned, but I didn't utter a sound. Dec hovered over me. "Hey. It's going to be okay."

I couldn't believe he, of all people, actually said those words. Nothing would be okay.

Shaking my head, I stared through him. "No. It's not. How can you say that?"

My voice was flat. My chest hollow.

Char stepped forward. "I can get you the best care. When you're ready, we can put you in touch with a prosthetic specialist. It's incredible the advancements they've made."

Her words stunned me. "You think I'm going to

get a metal replacement?"

Her mouth opened and closed a couple of times and her brow drew together. "Well, not right away but, I thought…"

"Yeah, well, don't think, Red. You don't know me or what I'll do."

Sadness fell like a shadow across her pretty features, and some sick part of me rejoiced in hurting her. People were quick to assume. Jesus. I still lay in the hospital and hadn't even come to grips with my loss, let alone planning new parts for my body. I didn't want to look like a freaking robot!

"I'll just wait outside," she whispered before shuffling out.

Dec grabbed a chair and pulled it over, sitting close.

"It sucks to be you, man. I'm not gonna lie. I didn't know what to expect when I walked in here. When I saw you only slightly banged up on your face, I figured maybe they'd exaggerated your injuries." He sighed heavily.

Turning my head to him, I ground out. "I can't do it."

"What? The whole prosthetic leg thing? Hey, you know Char was trying to help. She's a nurse. She's dealt with this sort of thing before."

And he figured that's what I was talking about? Char?

"No. Not that. I can't live as a cripple. A burden on the military. A burden on you. Char. Myself."

And that was the crux of it, wasn't it? I'd left myself down. Failed at the only thing I excelled at. I'd let my team down. There was nothing left for me.

Dec stood, coiled and in fight or flight mode. I'd seen it so often. I knew what was coming. He paced, rubbing the back of his neck. "You listen to me, you son of a bitch!" His voice came out loud. Realizing it and looking to the door as if expecting a nurse to come barreling in, he quieted down. "Don't give me any of this 'poor me' bullshit. It's not you. You're better than that. You're a soldier of war for the United States of America, for Christ's sake! You've protected your country. You've damn well protected me! That's more than most people on this planet can say. Now you might see this as the end, but fuck it, man. This is only the beginning. You're not a quitter. You have never been, and I'm going to make sure you don't start now. Ever. You hear me?"

He looked fierce in his deliverance of the very harsh truth. The fire in his eyes had ignited into a strong arsenal of power.

He strode to the bed, pissed as hell. "Who was it who stood by me when I didn't want to go on? Who got me through days so bad, I wanted to put a bullet through my skull? Hmm? Who was that? You think you get to lie there and make out like you got nothing to live for?"

Shaking his head, he walked to the window. "I guess I don't know you at all, my friend. I thought you had more fight than that. Guess I was wrong."

How dare he stand there and tell me that shit! His situation months ago was different than mine. He hadn't been blown the fuck apart. He had no right to get angry.

"Fuck you!" I spat, wishing I could punch something. My own temper spiked at my friend's admonishment. I thought I had his full support. Always. No matter what. Obviously not.

"You think I want the stares? The snickers? People talking behind my back? Not being able to look in the mirror without being reminded every single day of what I lost? You don't know anything!" I roared, and within seconds a doctor burst through the door, alarm on his face.

"Everything okay in here?"

"Everything's just dandy." I glowered at Dec.

"I was just leaving," he grumbled, returning my scowl. He stomped to the door and didn't look back as he left.

Now I really did feel sorry for myself. I'd pissed off the one person who swore he would have my back until the day he died. I truly was alone. And it had all happened in the space of a few minutes.

Chapter Twenty-Three

Char

"He's not doing too well, is he?" Silly question. Who wouldn't be after going through something so traumatic. Still, I worried if he'd ever get over it.

We sat in the back of the cab, heading for the hotel. He pondered my question and then sighed. "Normally, I'd say 'yeah, he's fine. Just pissed. He'll get over it, but this is different. Something in his eyes has changed. The fighting spirit he's always had. I couldn't see it. It's like it had been snuffed out. That's what concerns me more than anything."

My stomach rolled. For Viper's best friend to come to such a conclusion proved extremely serious. For once I hadn't taken the sting of his words to me too seriously. As much as his rebuttal hurt, it was to be expected. It was part of the process. I'd seen it before.

"So what now? Will you stay until he gets sent home?"

"I have to. I'm all he has. I want to be with him on his journey home. As angry as I am at his attitude right now, I won't leave him."

God. Loyal to the death. It touched me deeply. "He's so lucky to have you. I mean it. So is Mac."

I smiled as he glanced at me with a hint of a smirk. His jaw ticked.

"You jealous, Red?"

He'd never called me that before and somehow it didn't have the same kick as when Viper called me it. Barking out a laugh, I coughed. "Red, huh? Since when do you call me that?"

Shrugging, he chuckled. "I kinda like it." He held my focus. Perusing. Searching. "You're good for him, you know. He knows it. Mac and I know it. You just need to be patient."

Balking at his statement, I shook my head. "We've only just arrived at a place where we don't hate each other. And now this. I feel like we're back to square one. I don't know if he wants my help."

"Sure he does. His mind is just fucked right now. The one thing he's passionate about has been taken away. He's grieving. I can't imagine what he's going through. But don't give up on him. I've seen changes in him since you've uh, got under his skin…"

He full-on smiled now, looking at me and then out the window. The cab slowed down as we neared the hotel.

Punching him in the arm, I sang, "What's that supposed to mean?"

Too late. The cab had stopped and Dec was handing the driver some foreign money. Before I could punch him again, he was out the door, laughing as I swiped at the air where he'd been sitting.

After all the tension of the past hour, it felt good to laugh, although I knew it would be short-lived. I almost felt guilty at my change in mood while Viper lay in pieces and Mac stressed about the situation back home.

My cell pinged as I followed Dec inside. It showed a text from Mac. Waiting until we were in our separate rooms, I flung myself on the bed and read it.

Hey girl,
Just wanted to send my love. Hope Viper is doing okay. Let me know how things are going. Love you, Mac. XX

Hitting reply, I began to type.

He's lost his left leg from the knee down. I guess he's pretty lucky, considering. Mentally he's shutting down. I'll stay for a couple more days and head home. Your man is going to bring Viper home. Miss you.
Much love. Char. XX

A quick response came with a love heart. What more could be said? She needed to process his injury too. I didn't want to say too much. Dec needed to fill her in on the details, which hopefully he'd get more of tomorrow. We'd left in a hurry and hadn't been able to speak to anyone regarding

Viper's release.

How much leverage would my nursing status give us? Probably not much in a foreign country.

My mind drifted back to the broken soldier whose life flashed before his eyes and the rug pulled from under him. How would I react in the same situation?

I'd be happy to be alive, for a start. Losing half a leg didn't mean the end. He could do other things with his life. A prosthetic would mean better mobility. Not having to rely on crutches or a wheelchair. He had to see that. Was it up to me to show him? Perhaps. But ultimately, Viper would need to make his own choices about his recovery. A horse could be led to water but you couldn't make it drink.

My assault seemed like a dream now as I processed Viper's situation. As horrible as mine had been at the time and how it affected me, that took a backseat now. I had something far more serious to focus on. It seemed like a good thing, as bad as the whole scenario was. I pondered how Viper would gather his life back.

Other wounded soldiers recovered and took on different roles. If not in the military, then in different fields. Perhaps Dec and he could team up and do something.

I'd need to wait until he returned home to mention it again. His fragility right now could push him over the edge.

I wanted to visit again before I flew out, regardless as to whether he pushed me away. He needed to know I wasn't going anywhere.

I must have dozed because I awoke to a knocking at my door. A little dazed, I rose and checked the peephole.

Dec.

Checking my watch, I noted the time as six p.m. I must have slept fitfully.

Opening the door, and with his change of clothing, he ambled in. "You up for some dinner? I thought we could grab something out. Might as well see some of the town while we're here."

"Uh, I guess. Just let me get some other clothes on."

"You look fine. It won't be anywhere flash."

"Oh. Okay. Well then, I'll grab my shoes and we can go."

***

"Did you get a message from Mac?" I asked, after swallowing a mouthful of braised pork hock. Dec had ordered bratwurst with potato mash.

"I called her. She was at work on her break, luckily. She's pretty upset and concerned, but is remaining positive."

I could read his facial expressions. When he spoke of his love, his eyes gleamed. "You miss her already."

"Like crazy. I hate leaving her. When I thought I'd never see her again, it destroyed me."

"Like I said earlier, she's lucky. And no, I'm not jealous. I love Mac to bits. She deserves someone who adores her like you do."

"You wish you had the same thing."

203

"I didn't say that."

"You didn't need to. I can see it in your expressions."

"I've never wanted the whole long-term relationship thing, you know? I was always happy dating different guys. But after seeing what you have with my best friend, well, it's sickening, but also every girl's dream."

"It hasn't been easy. I was a dick for a while until I realized pushing her away wasn't the answer. I needed her too much. Viper and I are similar. He'll realize how much he cares for you too."

He kept saying it, but what if he didn't know his friend now that something life-changing had happened? And why was I stressing so much about it? We'd slept together. We hadn't committed to each other. I'd done casual so many times before and not worried about it.

The idea of not having Viper in my life sent razor-sharp stabs of pain into my chest.

Dec's phone pealed out and I couldn't help wondering if it was Mac.

With a frown between his eyebrows, he commanded, "Hello?" Silence. "Yep. Okay. I'll be there soon. I'm finishing dinner."

Placing the cell back in his jeans pocket, he must have sensed me watching him.

"The hospital said Viper's asking for me."

My eyes widened. "What do you suppose it's about?"

"Not sure, but I'll head on over after we eat. Do you mind if I go alone?"

"Not at all. I'll visit in the morning."

What could be so urgent to warrant a call from the hospital? Had he deteriorated and wanted Dec by his side?

Errant thoughts began again and I knew my time of relative calmness had ended. I'd be restless until I knew what was going on.

Chapter Twenty-Four

Viper

I needed to amend things with Dec. I'd been an asshole. I hated the tension between us. I hated knowing I'd sent him away angry.

At first, the hospital had refused my request, but upon demanding to see someone in charge and getting a little heated, they'd eventually relented. Visiting hours were almost finished, but I didn't care. I needed to see my brother.

Waiting proved hard. I wasn't sure he'd come after storming out. Perhaps he decided to let me cool off instead. And what about Char? Would she come? Part of me hoped so but the part that truly needed to atone for my behavior with Dec hoped not.

Nurses came and went. I remained on pain medication and had blood taken again. My drip had been changed twice. The catheter remained.

When the door opened, I assumed it was Dec, but I sucked in a hard breath when a nurse walked in with a wheelchair. I'd forgotten about the doctor wanting me up and out of bed today. I'd assumed it would have happened earlier, but I guess they'd been busy. I hadn't seen this nurse before. She appeared to be around twenty-something with mousy hair pulled up into a bun. Nice looking, but she had nothing on my Red. *My Red.* Shit. Listen to me. She wasn't mine. I hadn't earned her. Nor would I get to keep her now. The idea of that saddened me way more than it should.

"Hello. I'm Eva. I'm here to get you up and about."

I'd said no wheelchairs! "You got any crutches?"

"We do, but I've been told to get you sitting in the chair before we tackle the crutches. I need to remove your catheter first."

Oh crap. The muscles in my legs tightened as she moved toward the bed, donning a pair of gloves.

I squeezed my eyes closed.

"You may feel a little sting."

Yeah, when a doctor or nurse said that, it normally hurt like hell. Funny, considering what I'd been through. Getting a small, plastic tube taken out should be a piece of cake.

I felt the blankets get pulled down.

The nurse giggled. "It's not that bad. You don't need to worry."

Opening one eye, I squinted at her face, not able to lean up and watch. I was a complete wuss when it came to medical procedures.

I felt a gentle tug and a burning sensation. I gritted my teeth against it.

"All done," she chirped.

"That's it?" I asked, fully opening my eyes, deciding it hadn't been so bad after all.

"Yep. You may experience an uncomfortable bladder for a couple of days and a small amount of blood in your urine, but it's normal. It should settle soon."

I'm glad she told me because if I relieved myself and saw any sign of blood, it would set off the panic button.

Settling into the mattress again, I waited until she finished tidying up the tray one of the other nurses had wheeled in earlier and her gloves had been removed.

"Now. Let's get you out of this bed."

Ah. No. "I'm not getting in that chair." My voice boomed and she startled, halfway to the chair.

"You don't want to get up?" she asked meekly.

"I do, but I want crutches."

"Doctor's orders."

"Fuck doctor's orders. I'm not getting in that chair."

She glared at me and strode out. Probably to get her superior, but she could bring the President of the United States in and it wouldn't change my decision.

Sitting in that chair, which sat facing me like some freaking torture device, would show everyone I was disabled.

Who was I kidding? Crutches wouldn't hide the gaping hole where my foot used to be. It would just make me seem less…helpless.

Eva pushed open my door again with a male in tow. He appeared middle-aged and wore a scowl.

Jackass. If he thought he could persuade me, let him try.

No doctor was going to give me orders that didn't directly affect my health.

"You don't want to get in the wheelchair? Why?"

He stayed back with the nurse at a safe distance. Intelligent man.

"I don't need it. I can use crutches just fine."

The doctor and nurse shared a knowing look before he responded. "Ultimately, it's your choice. Nurse, bring in some crutches."

That didn't take much persuading. Thankful for the doctor's understanding, I gave him a nod.

"We need to get you into a sitting position." He moved to my bed and picked up a remote which I didn't know existed and pushed a button. My bed began rising so I ascended upward until I could begin swinging my body around so my right leg hung over the edge.

"Are you in any pain?" Doc asked.

My thigh ached, but apart from that, I couldn't feel much. A wooziness slipped through my head, so I paused to let it pass.

Thank God the catheter had been removed for this exercise, even though the drip remained. I wasn't sure how I'd be able to walk on crutches plus maneuver the metal stand it hung from.

The doctor must have noticed where my attention was. "Nurse Eva will walk with you to help keep you steady and to keep you attached to your IV bag."

Speaking of her, she breezed in with crutches in

tow. Her happy persona was back in place, perhaps because she didn't have to deal with my attitude any further.

Placing them in front of me, I gripped my lifeline, hoisting myself up and settling them under my arms. I wobbled as another wave of vertigo hit me, causing me to sway and my vision to distort. Two sets of arms grabbed me.

"That's why we prefer the chair for the first time," offered the doctor smugly.

Not deterred and not wanting to prove him correct, I shook off the dizziness and put all my weight on my good leg, letting my stump dangle. A heaviness pulled at the base of it, probably all the blood rushing south. I hoped that didn't cause it to start bleeding again.

"Do you need me to stay, nurse?"

"No. Thank you. I can handle it."

The doctor nodded, wheeling the chair into the corner of the room, probably hoping I'd fail at the crutches and have to use it, but I'd be damned if I'd give him the satisfaction.

It's not like I hadn't used crutches before. As uncomfortable as they felt resting in my armpits, I needed to get out of the confined space of the sterile room.

With slow precision, I closed the gap to the door, stopping so Eva could open it to let me out. She kept in step with me because of the IV stand, making sure the leads didn't get tangled.

It felt good to be using my arms again. To be vertical. The hospital outside my room was like another world. I'd only heard the sounds and voices and not seen who they were coming from or what made such discord.

Talk about a hive of activity. Soldiers in uniforms paraded up and down hallways. The injured were led or walked themselves to wherever it was they needed to get to. Medical staff went about their tasks like busy worker bees. It seemed all hospitals were the same, no matter where you were.

"Just take it slowly at first. You'll tire quickly, so we won't go far."

Not listening to her, I let the long hallway lead me away from my prison, surprisingly in better spirits at being able to move about. Being in this place, I was just like every other patient. I'd been injured in battle. I didn't stand out. I blended in, bringing about a certain amount of comfort. Stepping out into the real world would be what rattled me. I wasn't looking forward to it at all. In fact, it brought with it a stomach full of nausea.

I hated the feeling of no foot and lower leg. I'd suffered several breaks in my lifetime, but still, I'd been able to feel it there. Now, my left stump simply dangled.

"You're doing great." The nurse had a hard time keeping up with me. My arms needed the exercise as much as my leg, but I found after doing one round of the ward, I grew extremely weary. I still had painkillers pumping through my blood, which didn't help the fatigue. Plus, my body had barely begun recuperating in the short time since the accident.

Staff barely glanced up from their busy

schedules. I proved to be just another number in the system. Some men and women of war wandered the halls, nodding their heads or smiling as we passed, a knowing glint in their eye that they understood what I was going through.

I sighed out, some of the weight I carried easing away. Perhaps I could do this after all.

A soldier appeared from around a corner with his whole leg missing. He too battled crutches. We found each other's gaze and seemed to pause momentarily as if bonding over our similar injuries, his far worse than mine.

"Landmine?" he asked.

The nurse stopped beside me as I took a pause. "Yeah. You?"

"Yep. Nearly lost an arm too, but they managed to save it. Just damn thankful to be alive."

My eyes widened. "Jesus. That's great they could save it."

He nodded and began to move forward. "Room 85 if you need someone to talk to. Name's Zane."

"Viper."

We moved on, Zane's words playing on a loop in my head. *I'm just damn thankful to be alive.*

He'd lost his entire right leg and yet, he seemed okay. My lower leg was gone and I wanted to give up. My earlier meltdown seemed trivial and stupid.

Another guy passed us. Looked like he'd lost an eye. One arm hung in a sling and he had a deep, stitched wound from his ear, down into the shirt he wore. Fuck!

I sucked in a breath when he still managed to smile at me and my nurse. Was I the only asshole fucked up by his injury? These men, worse than me, somehow coped. Or did they? Were their smiles simply for show? Were they so traumatized by what had happened to them that they too wanted to give up?

War screwed everyone up. The scars on the outside healed, but the ones on the inside never did. Soldiers committed suicide every day because they lived in their own messed up heads. True heroes no one ever heard about. Their names never got plastered on the news. Yet, celebrities grabbed the spotlight for breaking a heel on a shoe or changing their hair color. Nothing could be more insane.

Reaching my room, I halted. A voice I knew better than any, boomed from nearby.

"How long do you think he'll be?"

I couldn't hear the nurse's reply.

Dec. He'd come.

As tired as I'd become, I needed to let him know I was back. I glanced at Eva. "Just a minute. There's someone here to see me." I motioned with my hand up the corridor.

"I really should get you back in bed. You've done more than enough for today."

Shaking my head, I began moving, giving her no choice but to follow. "Not happening yet."

I strode to where the voice had come from, turning a corner, the nurse's station coming in to view.

Dec's broad back faced me as he leaned against the large workstation.

"Hey, man," I called out as we neared.

He spun and grinned, seeing me up and about.

"Wow. Look at you rocking those crutches. Good to see, brother." His eyes moved to Eva, crinkling at the corners as he offered her a bigger smile.

Walking to us, he said, "I got here and wondered where you were. I hoped you hadn't been transferred or sent home already."

"Nah. I'll be here for another few days."

Dec followed us as we traipsed back to my room. As much as I hated the confinement, my body rejoiced at being able to lie back down.

Eva helped me onto the bed and positioned the IV pole back before disappearing again. Visiting hours had officially finished, but allowances had been made after I'd insisted my friend be let in for a short time. What I needed to say wouldn't take long, but couldn't wait.

"How does it feel to be able to move around?" he asked, pulling back the chair he'd sat on earlier.

"To be honest, it's okay. Well, here in the hospital, anyway. I don't grab anyone's attention because most patients here are pretty severely injured."

"But..."

He sensed my *but* coming. And there was a *but*.

"Back home will be different. Going out. Being in public. I don't want the pity or stares."

"Is that what has you in a flap? You're worried about what others think? Since when has that bothered you?"

We were heading back into a heated discussion and I didn't want that. I'd asked him to come to apologize, so I didn't let him know what bothered me about it. Instead, I let out a long exhale and rubbed my face.

"I know. Look, forget it, okay? That's not why I asked you to come. I wanted to say I'm sorry about the way I carried on earlier."

Dec laughed. Fully. "You got me back here just to apologize? Man, you don't need to do that. Look at what has happened to you. I'd be pretty irate and down on myself too in your shoes. It's okay."

"Still, I acted like a dick." Reaching over to the bedside cabinet, I poured myself a plastic cup full of water and took a swig, my mouth suddenly dry.

"So, you feeling any better? Moving about must have helped."

How did I answer him? Was I better? No. I'd never be better, but seeing others like myself eased some of the burden.

"I don't know how the fuck to feel. I mean, this…" I pointed to my leg. "This is forever. I'd rather the landmine took me altogether."

"Shut it, bro. Don't talk like that. You think it would be easy for me to lose you? For Char or Mac? Do you think your parents would have wanted that?"

Pain shot from his eyes and I knew I was being selfish, but he didn't have to live in my shoes.

Hearing him speak about my folks spread guilt and sorrow further into my marrow. Perhaps if they were still alive I'd be coping better. I couldn't be sure.

Finishing the cup of water, I fell back onto the bed. "I miss them."

"They'd be so proud of you. They were anyway."

I wished I could talk to them again. Listen to their advice. Hear their voices. My dad pushing me forward. My mom with her gentle way, hugging me and telling me all would be well.

Nothing else compared. As much as I loved Dec and he had replaced my blood family, it still wasn't the same. But they were gone and I had to deal with the loss. Would have to deal with it every day for the rest of my life.

I knew they'd want me to remain strong and make the best of things, but it was so damn hard.

"I know."

Dec wasn't one to dwell on a subject too long. "So, when do you think they'll release you?"

"In the next few days, apparently."

"I'm staying. I'll fly home with you."

"I've got a military escort. You don't need to. Go be with Mac. Take Char home."

"Ain't happening, man. Whether you like it or not, I'm here until you leave. Already discussed it with Char and she's happy to fly solo."

Red. She'd never been far from my thoughts. The woman who had flown all the way here to see me and I'd been a dick to her too.

I'd need to right that wrong when I arrived back in the States.

Chapter Twenty-Five

Char

I hadn't seen Viper again. I'd decided to give him space. Dec had visited alone again and remained behind.

Sitting, contemplating everything out the aircraft window, I weighed up where I stood in Viper's life. If I stood at all.

What was it about this guy that had me tied in knots? I'd deliberated over this so many times and I couldn't put my finger on it. It was a feeling. A strange pull deep down that had a hold on my emotions. More than physical. Even though he was a specimen to behold without clothes, to me, even with half his leg gone, he'd still be whole. It didn't matter. It didn't take away his presence or energy. The man who'd put it all on the line for his country. The man who'd saved me from me, just by being there.

If he thought he could push me away, he was wrong. I knew we could have something amazing.

For the first time in my life, I wanted it all with one man. Perhaps I'd known since I'd first laid eyes on him at University Hospital when Mac had been abducted. But seeing him in Germany, so desolate and in pain, strengthened my resolve. Like Dec, I wouldn't walk away. No matter what. This man was the *more* I craved. Even when he put up all his walls to push me away. Snippets of my meltdown after being accosted out front of my home, when I'd been barely functioning as Viper carried me from his bathroom into the bedroom. He'd let that wall crumble for an instant, showing me the compassionate man underneath. He could be that man again. I could bring him back. I wanted to try.

I dozed on and off, never truly falling into fitful sleep. The flight seemed endless before touching down in Detroit.

As good as if felt being home again, I hated the thought of Viper being a world away. Did he think he'd succeeded in pushing me away upon learning of my departure home? It didn't matter. I had a few days to gather myself, get back to work, and prepare for the storm I knew was brewing.

After retrieving my suitcase, on my way to the car rental counter, I stopped short. Standing not ten feet away from me was Mac. A huge smile lit her face.

What the hell? What was she doing here?

Happy to see her face, I dropped my bag and almost skipped to my best friend.

We embraced. A hug I'd never forget. It didn't need to be followed up with words of any kind. The fierceness of it held way more than words ever could.

She'd come as my support. I'd gone to Germany to support Dec and Viper and now she came to offer it to me.

A tear leaked from my eye. This girl was everything to me. A true warrior in her own right.

Pulling back, I watched her own tears fall.

"I thought you might need a ride back home."

Laughing at her, I said, "Really, Mac? You drove all this way to drive me home?"

"I missed you. Plus, I was going stir crazy in my apartment."

Picking up my bag, we left the busy airport and walked to her Mustang. I had a lot to tell her.

Glad I could sit back and talk while she drove, I got settled and began.

I relayed first seeing Viper. Dec's reaction. The anger he'd directed at me. She'd been through it all, so who better to understand?

"Stubborn men. You know it's just a cry for help, right?" She turned onto Interstate 94.

"Yeah, I think I've worked that out."

"He's going to need you in the coming weeks and months. It won't be easy, but trust me, stick with it and you'll be rewarded with his trust and undying devotion."

Glancing at her wistful expression, I knew she referred to her and Dec, but in many ways, the two soldiers were as alike as true brothers.

"I hear what you're saying. I thought about it on the flight back. The damn man has burrowed so far under my skin, I don't think I could walk away if I wanted to."

"I hear ya." She sighed. "If you need advice, I can't promise it will be the right advice, but I can promise it will be honest."

"Thanks, girl. You know I love you, right?"

"I know. Back at ya, sister."

We arrived back at Mac's apartment in just over an hour with traffic thick out of Detroit.

"Can you drop me home after I grab my stuff? I think I'm ready to move back into my apartment."

She turned quickly. "You sure? You don't have to. You're welcome to stay with me as long as you need."

"No. You know what? I'm ready. I have to do this. After seeing what Viper has gone through and will continue to go through, I need to toughen up and deal with my fears. I'll be okay."

She still didn't look convinced, but simply nodded. "I'll help you pack."

It was midday on Wednesday. I quickly realized my friend should be working.

"Ah, why aren't you at work?"

We entered her apartment. I had left my suitcase in the car and placed my purse on the small table beside the door.

"I bribed Cassie to cover for me. I'm pulling a double tomorrow."

She made it sound like no big deal, but for her to do that for me, meant so much.

I moved to her and pulled her into another hug. "You're the best. You didn't have to do that. I know how hard double shifts are."

"Eh, don't sweat it. Working helps me keep busy while Dec's away."

"Well, I'm going to make it up to you. For being here for me. Letting me stay. I'll organize a girl's weekend away where we can be pampered."

"I'd like that."

***

Trudging up to the apartment I'd called home for the last couple of years, it appeared the same, yet different. I didn't feel any attachment toward it like I had in the past. Now it was merely a place where I would continue to live until I decided to move on. The personal emotions attached to it were gone—leaving the moment I was assaulted.

Mac touched my arm as I paused. "You okay?"

"Yeah. Just realizing I haven't missed it. That it might be time to move somewhere new soon. Make a fresh start."

"Sometimes it's what we have to do in order to move forward."

Another shift happened at that moment. Maybe I'd been stuck in a rut for so long it had taken a couple of scary incidents to shake my world. To jerk me into breaking free from my mold. I'd existed in my comfort zone for far too long. Meeting Viper had pulled me from that, and it was as if the shift I felt was my soul rejoicing.

Opening the door on my old life, I boldly crossed the threshold, Mac dragging one large suitcase and me lugging the other.

Inside everything remained the same. Yet I had changed. Opening the blinds, I let light in, the sun finding its way across the floor to my familiar couch with the same tan cushions sitting where I'd left them. The timber-framed painting of an autumn landscape no longer held its appeal.

Mac perched on the recliner facing my television, looking at me while I surveyed my surroundings.

"Strange being home?"

"Yeah. It's weird. I feel like I don't belong here anymore."

"Maybe you don't."

Chapter Twenty-Six

Viper

It had been a cruel week of ups and downs. Dec kept his promise and barely left my side. Each day, I'd hobbled on crutches down the lengths of the hospital hallways, itching to get out of my room. The confined space, although hiding me from revealing my stumpy limb, did my head in. I felt caged. Entombed.

The day of my release spoke of freedom and a whole world of fear. Two opposite emotions sparring with each other. My armpits ached from the crutches, but it was nothing compared to the ache inside. The constant conflict with my emotions.

Instead of traveling with a military partner, I'd been allowed to travel with Dec after a consultation with the higher-ups. They knew and trusted Dec and knew I'd be in safe hands.

"You ready to head home?" he asked in the back of the cab.

My wound apparently had been healing well, considering. I'd been discharged with a ton of bandages and pain meds if I needed them…on the stipulation that I visit with the hospital daily to get my bandages changed.

"Truth be told, I'm not sure." Glancing down at my left leg and the way it jutted out from the seat left the chasm inside wider. I still needed to come to grips with my new look. Not seeing my calf and foot.

After speaking with Zane for an hour or so in the hospital and him leaving me his number for when he returned to the States, I wasn't feeling quite as sorry for myself. I'd make sure to call him. Keep in touch with someone who could relate.

"I'm gonna stay with you for a bit. Until you feel more comfortable and can get around easier."

Feeling like a charity case, I gritted my teeth. "You don't need to do that. I'll be fine."

"Like fuck you will. I'm staying. End of story. You can bust my ass all you want, but you need someone with you. Stop being so damn stubborn and let me help."

His voice brooked no argument, even though I could push it. He'd do what he felt was right, regardless of my opinion.

"Whatever, man."

"You're not fighting me on this?"

"What's the point? You're just as stubborn as me. Sounds like you've made your mind up."

"Good."

And that was that. Dec would be moving in.

"Mac okay with it?"

"She's fine. In fact, she's the one who suggested it?"

"She did?"

"Uh huh. She cares about you."

Blowing air between my compressed lips, I peered out the window. I needed to let more people in and accept their help. That included Red.

I wouldn't be able to hide from her. She'd be at the damn hospital every day, making sure I obeyed protocol and doctor's orders.

I remembered the horrified expression on her face when the nurse had thrown the bed covers down to reveal my injury. She'd schooled it well after a heartbeat, but I'd noticed. Deep down beneath the cool, professional façade I'd seen fear. Shock. Pity. All of it.

I imagined her thoughts at that moment. *Oh, my God. He's lost some of his leg. He'll never be the same again. What does his future hold now? He'll have to quit the military. What will he do? How will he cope? Will he be able to have a relationship?*

They were the exact same questions I'd asked myself and I didn't have answers to any of them.

***

Stepping foot back in my house brought me to a complete stop. Someone had been here and redecorated. Not the furniture. In the living room against the wall above the couch hung a large, Welcome Home banner. On the coffee table below sat some fresh flowers in a vase, and above floated a sea of black and white balloons.

What the actual fuck? My jaw hung slack. Dec smiled guiltily at my reaction, obviously having a hand in it. I didn't know whether to be pissed that someone had been in my place while I'd been out of the country or happy that they'd gone to the effort. The balloons and banner signified a happy return as if a celebration should be occurring. Like it was my frigging birthday or something.

I didn't feel that at all. Coming home scared the crap out of me. It signaled the end of my career. The end of everything I'd known. Frowning, I threw a glare at Dec.

"You did this?"

"Well, not physically. It was Char's idea. She thought it might cheer you up, so I agreed."

When he noticed my not so happy reaction, his smile dwindled.

"You're mad?"

I went to shove a hand through my hair and a crutch fell to the floor, causing me to almost lose my balance. I had to hop on my right leg to stabilize. Dec grabbed my arm.

"Easy, man. I got you."

He bent down and picked up the crutch after he was sure I wouldn't topple.

At that one simple moment, a flick switched in my head again. A surge of anger rose. I couldn't even stand properly by myself. I was helpless. Useless.

I rushed to the couch, throwing myself down, feeling a throb at my injury site. Throwing one of the crutches across the room, I let out a growl.

Dec stood in place, quietly observing. I sucked in

air. In. Out. In. Out. I needed to destroy something and I think he knew it.

Gripping both sides of my scalp, I squeezed. "Fuck this shit! I can't even stand on my own two Goddam feet! I need a babysitter!"

My chest tightened. I'd never needed anyone, being independent from a young age. Even as a boy and an only child, I'd done things around the house. My parents had made sure I could cook, clean, and sew buttons on before I reached puberty.

Suddenly the weight of everything came crashing through me. The reality of never being able to fight. I'd struggled to mesh with civilian life for years since joining the military, which was why I'd always accepted every mission offered to me. How in God's name would I do it? I needed the thrill of battle as much as the beat of my heart.

Pounding my fist into my right thigh, I let out a roar. It sounded more like a dying bear. I could relate. A part of me was dying. A slow, painful demise of who I'd always been and could never be again.

A hand came to my shoulder. I hadn't seen or felt Dec move to sit beside me.

He didn't speak. Simply squeezed and didn't let go while I bled tears from my soul. Sobs of grief. Despair. My dark warrior beast wanted to jump out and kill. Maim. What would I do with him now? I'd have to tamp him down. I had no outlet. I couldn't even stand on two feet, let alone tear anything to shreds.

Dec's cell rang. He rose and I vaguely heard him say, "Hey angel…" The pounding of blood in my ears drowned out the rest as he moved away, leaving me to teeter on the edge of hell.

My mind felt like it was spiraling out of control as I grabbed a cushion and threw it across the room, a picture of my parents hitting the wooden floor and smashing.

I didn't care in that moment, my rage cresting into an entity of its own. I cursed multiple times, pushing myself off the couch, teetering. Lifting the one crutch I had, I thrust it under my arm and attempted to hobble into my room where my handgun rested, inside my bedside drawer. I needed the soothing feel of metal to help calm me. Even just to hold it.

My shoulders banged on the hallway wall as I struggled to push on. Dec would be sure to hear me and cut his call short. I just needed to get a few more feet to my room so I could shut the door.

I hadn't even bothered to try picking up my other crutch. I was too high on adrenalin and sorrow to care. I braced a hand on the wall and used it as leverage to propel myself forward.

"Viper?"

Dec stood in the living room, phone still to his ear as his expression became one of intensity. As if he knew my plans. We stood for a long drawn out second. My brother. My family. I tried to relay how much he meant to me as a strange calm fell over me. I gave him a nod and with one final thrust forward, I turned and entered my room, closing the door and locking it.

Dec cursed and followed down the hallway.

"Viper? You okay? Talk to me. What are you

doing?" His desperate plea failed to pull me from getting my weapon.

As I overthought everything and the sorrow deepened, the idea flourished. Holding my gun wouldn't be enough. It would signify further all I had lost. Suddenly the road ahead I had to travel seemed endless. I couldn't do it. It was too hard. My feelings of doom in the hospital returned and all I wanted was peace. I needed the hurt to end.

One jump. Two. Dropping the crutch and sitting on my bed, I pulled the bottom drawer open and threw out my neatly folded shorts. My breathing belied my inner calm when only moments ago chaos had nourished my veins.

Eyeing my lifeline, I reached in and gripped the cold handle, peace reaching tentacles around my hand and up my arm.

Pounding on the door. "Come on, brother. Open the door! Talk to me! What do you need?"

What did I need? Funny thing about despair. It was a lonely street. Nothing anyone said could make it better. I needed the torture in my head to stop. I needed to feel whole again.

My other hand came to caress the short barrel. My friend. The only thing I knew could take the torment away.

Cocking the chamber, I breathed out when I found it full. Not that I needed them all. One would do.

They say in the moments before death, your life flashes before your eyes. The good parts and the bad. All on a continuous movie feed as you take your final breaths. I had nothing but numbness.

Black.

The door shook from Dec's weight.

"You better open this fucking door right now or I'm breaking it down!"

A second ticked by. A second closer to ending the excruciating torment. Without my career I was nothing. I lived for the missions which continued to feed my sickness. When I fought and let the warrior take over, I was somebody. I was focused and complete. I'd never get to experience that ever again. I'd have to try and fit into a society that I'd long since stopped being a part of. Regular folk didn't understand the struggles of trying to live back in normalcy after living off the grid in the desert with nothing but orders, chaos, and violence.

More seconds ticked by. Red's face flashed before me. She'd cry over my death. But she'd get over it. She'd survive. Life for her would go on the way it always had. I couldn't give her what she wanted. What she needed. To think for even a second that I could be the man she deserved was simply wishful thinking. She didn't know the true depths of my mental state. I would only hurt her more by living. She had feelings for me. I knew. And under the right circumstances, I'd probably grip on to that with both hands, but nothing about me was normal. Not now.

The banging continued, and in another couple of pushes, Dec would be though.

I eyed my trusty revolver. We'd been through a lot together so it proved fitting that it should be the weapon to put me out of my misery.

Dec's frantic screaming faded and a calm

washed over me as I raised the gun to my temple. Soon. Mom and Dad. Soon.

Closing my eyes and taking a couple of full deep breaths, the first I'd been able to since my injury, I squeezed the trigger.

Chapter Twenty-Seven

Viper

A click. Nothing. I pressed the trigger again. Same thing. What the fuck? Pulling my gun down to check it, a loud bang sounded as Dec finally managed to push the door in.

It reverberated off the wall, causing me to pause and look up. That's all the time took to gauge my friend's horrified face.

In an instant he ran across the room, a roar sounding from his thick throat. "Are you fucking insane?"

He practically launched himself at me, snatching the gun away, not caring that it now pointed at him.

Once it left my hands, everything slowed down. Dec's words became vacant and slurred like I floated in a big bowl of soup. My torso began tingling and the room tilted.

I felt two hands grip my shoulders seconds too late. The welcome darkness came.

***

The darkness didn't stay. Light seeped in. My eyelids fluttered. Shapes morphed. Sounds intensified. Brain fog held tight as I attempted to gain my bearings. Images flashed.

Gun at my temple. Door thumping and bulging at the hinges.

Am I dead? I don't feel dead. Aren't I meant to be floating? Weightless?

My body feels…heavy.

"He's coming around."

That voice. Feminine. Captivating. Familiar.

"Can I have a moment?"

"Sure. I'll be outside."

Feet padding away.

Lifting my heavy lids, I focused on my surroundings. A room. Sterile. Similar to one I'd been in recently. Hospital.

My neck pivoted to a shadow looming. Green, scorching eyes plummeted me into an emotional tangle.

Burnished coppery strands of hair framed a heart-shaped face. Dotted freckles peppered an upturned nose which rested above sultry lips.

Worry marked her brow with a heavy indent.

"Hey." A quiet caress dragged feathery fingers along my psyche. Soothing.

"Hey." My reply sounded cracked and raspy.

"You scared the hell out of me. Not to mention Dec. He's been frantic."

"What happened?" I needed to know how I still lived? My gun had been loaded. Safety off.

Had Dec reached me in time?

Her bottom lip quivered, eyes cast downward before rising to meet mine again. "The gun. It jammed."

It did? My trusty pistol had failed? It had never let me down. Why now?

Too smart for her own good, she said, "You seem disappointed."

"I guess I am. It could have all been over. Now…I have to live with…this." Pointing at my leg under the blankets, I then aimed a finger at my head. "And this."

Silence ensued while she processed my admission. Her pupils eclipsed those chartreuse irises I swam in. "You want to die?" A whisper. Nothing more.

I watched on as her eyes welled but no liquid fell. Her strength wouldn't let it fall and I admired her for it. She wouldn't give me her tears. I didn't deserve them.

Unable to answer, I turned and stared at a curtained window.

The nurse taking care of me returned, quietly stepping up to my bed, assessing the situation. Char was in her uniform, obviously working. She must have taken time out to come visit me when she heard the news I'd been brought in.

"I'd better get back to my wing and do some more rounds. Look after him, Denise."

"I sure will. And I'll also let you know if there's any change."

Still, I couldn't look at her. I didn't want her disappointment. I'd already had her pity.

Now she truly might realize how screwed up and wrong for her I was. She needed to walk away.

Chapter Twenty-Eight

Char

God! I had been so close to bursting into tears back there. What had he been thinking? Did he feel so alone and beaten down that he wanted to kill himself? The image of him aiming the gun at his skull wouldn't leave me. Dec hadn't gone into too much detail but it had been enough to crack my heart in two. After having a barrel aimed at my skull, and the fear I'd felt, I couldn't help but wonder if he'd felt any of that same fear. Obviously not. Because to pull the trigger there had to be no fear.

I understood his anger and bereavement after losing part of his leg. I'd seen the myriad of emotions play out in patients before, but to want to die over it? There had to be way more going on in his head that we weren't aware of. PTSD was a silent killer in many cases. Most harbored their demons alone. Well, he wasn't pulling that shit again. Not while I still had breath left in me. And

I'm pretty sure Dec and Mac felt the same.

Walking to the waiting area, I greeted my friends solemnly. Mac had been crying and Dec…he looked pissed. And defeated.

Seeing his best friend in such a state would haunt him forever.

Mac stood as I approached and Dec gripped the seat harder, muscles bunching everywhere.

"How is he?" Mac choked.

Hugging her, I answered, "He's awake."

"And?" Dec stood and moved closer.

I took pause not really knowing what to say to them. "I don't know. He seems disappointed the gun jammed."

"Fuck!" Dec spit out a little too loudly for a hospital. A doctor and nurse walking by turned and stared before shuffling past. The three people waiting alongside them watched closely.

Mac appeased him by rubbing his back. "Keep your voice down! Be mindful of where you are."

He gripped the back of his neck, searching the area for anyone else staring. "I'm just so angry with him right now. I knew he'd struggle with what happened, but I didn't think…" Dragging in a breath, he pivoted and walked away, probably to get his head together.

"Do you think he'll try it again?" Mac asked, eyes glassy.

"He'll be on suicide watch for thirty-six hours. A psych will go in and evaluate him. Possibly change him to different anti-depressants. After that, we're gonna have to watch him like a hawk. There's only so long we can keep him here. The rest will be up to him."

As if thinking as she stared through me and then focused, she said, "I know it's horrible to say, but maybe it's a good thing he can't get around easily. It'll be harder for him to try anything stupid. We'll just have to make sure his weapons are locked away and anything he might be able to use instead. He can move in with us."

"No!" I shot out. "I'd like to help. I'll stay with him."

Mac appeared surprised, her brows rising. "What about work?"

"We'll figure something out between the three of us. Maybe Dec can watch him during the day until I get home."

"You don't have to do this, Char. I know how you feel about him. And I realize the state of his mind. Do you think Dec would be better at handling it?"

Probably. But I wasn't budging with this. I needed to show him I didn't care about his injuries. I cared about him.

If I moved back in for a bit, he wouldn't be able to avoid me. He'd have to face the fact that I wasn't going anywhere.

"Listen, I've got to get back to work. You back on the roster tomorrow?" I asked her, knowing she'd taken the day off to be with Dec.

"Yeah. I'll see you in the morning."

As I began stepping away, she touched my arm. "Thanks, Char. I mean it. You're going over and above. He'll realize it sooner or later."

She smiled. I walked away. I needed to focus on

my work and not on the stupidly, frustratingly, beautiful soldier who lay in ruins not far away. How could I save him?

Picking up a file from the nurse's station, an idea came to me.

Chapter Twenty-Nine

Viper

Two days. Two fucking days of being cooped up again under constant surveillance. Talk about feeling like a prisoner. A psychologist had visited twice. After appeasing her that I wasn't going to off myself again, she booked me for weekly sessions at her office and left. My head resembled a swirling eddy in constant motion. Doctors came. Nurses went. The cycle never stopped.

Red visited when she could, which was the only thing I looked forward to. My light in the absolute darkness. Staff treated me like I was some fragile freaking mental patient. I wasn't mental. I knew exactly what I wanted and that was for the pain to stop. Pain in the form of my memories. Pain in the form of needing it all to disappear. Did that make me a fruitcake? Perhaps. Dec and Mac popped in separately, Mac on nurse duty in a different ward, and Dec stopped by pretending like nothing had changed. I admired him for attempting to act normal.

On Friday, the third day, Red walked in at five p.m. dressed in jeans, a white fitted tee, and a large smile on her face.

"It's time to go, Sunshine," she sang.

"What? Go where? Home?" My spirits lifted. Could I be finally getting out of the hospital?

"You're coming with me. Not home. Just away from here." Her cryptic answer had silent questions bouncing around in my already too full brain, but I didn't voice them. I'd go anywhere with her to escape my room.

"So…they're letting me go. Just like that?"

"I've taken care of it." She moved to the bed with my crutches. The IV had been removed earlier in the day and my wound redressed.

As I dragged the sheets away and looked down at my missing limb, I asked, "What about getting the bandages on this replaced daily? You driving me here tomorrow? And the day after that?"

"Don't need to. I'm a nurse, remember? I have supplies."

Just what was she planning? The gleam in her eye held excitement. I guess I'd wait and see.

Swinging over the edge of the bed as best I could, I gripped the crutches and leveraged myself upright. She crowded me like a mother cat.

"It's okay. I've got this." It came out a little grouchy, but I didn't like to be coddled. She should know that.

I began to inch forward but stopped when Char opened the metal drawers beside the bed, pulling out my cell.

"It was in the pocket of your jeans when you were brought in."

"Oh. Okay. Thanks." I'd forgotten all about it.

We slowly crawled down the hallways, Char waving goodbye to her colleagues, telling them to have a good weekend. They'd go out. Party. Spend time with families. Relax. Do whatever the fuck they wanted. Me? I'd probably be getting transferred from one prison into another. Visions of Char taking me to her apartment so she could monitor me flashed through my brain. I didn't want to be treated like a helpless moron.

The new meds I'd been put on made my head cloudy. Today I'd awoken a little confused and spacey.

Reaching Red's SUV, she opened the door and again went to help me in. I stopped her immediately.

"I've got it! I can do this!" I barked at her, immediately sorry when I eyed her crestfallen expression.

"I'm just trying to help."

"I know, and I appreciate it, but I don't need it. If I do, I'll ask for it."

Hopping closer to the passenger seat, I gripped the overhead handle and hoisted my body onto the seat, thankful my right leg was still intact. It took some maneuvering, but I settled in, shutting the door as Char walked to the driver's side with a sour face.

A sliver of fire in my veins had me rejoicing at the normalcy of our exchange, at her reaction to my snarky tone. This was how we began.

I watched her closely as she slammed her door and threw the car into gear. Damn, if it didn't almost make me smile. For just an instant things felt…normal.

***

We'd missed the turnoff to my house so it grew pretty clear we weren't headed there. When the turnoff to Char's came and went, I had to ask. "Ahh, just where are we going? I'm not exactly dressed for an outing."

I wore an old pair of jeans and a shirt Dec had brought by on one of his visits. Apart from that, I had nothing else. If we were going to Char's I'd need more clothes.

Glancing in the back, Char skewed me a sideways smirk. Her earlier anger at me seemed to have eased somewhat. "All taken care of. Dec packed a bag for you."

Swinging around I found my large duffle bag on the seat. I was packed so full, it bulged. Pivoting back to the vague woman driving who looked like the cat who had caught the mouse, I asked, "Why do I need so many clothes? Cut the crap, woman, and tell me where I'm going."

I'd just been released from the hospital after attempting to blow my brains out. I didn't exactly feel like going on a trip, even if it were just to her apartment.

"Oh, stop being a baby. If you must know, we're going to my parents' cabin at Pinckney. It's surrounded by trees and backs onto a lake."

Seriously? Oh, my God. Barking out a laugh, I shot, "You have got to be kidding me? You want to take me into the wild? Like this?"

Pointing at the space where my leg was missing, I glared at her.

Not daring to meet my gaze, she cringed and looked back to the road. "It'll help you relax."

"Relax?" Laughing some more, I had to hand it to her. She knew how to push my buttons without even trying. "You expect me to relax as if I don't have a care in the world?"

Her cheeks reddened. Whether from anger or regret, I couldn't tell.

Her knuckles whitened as she gripped the wheel. Definitely anger. Little Miss Spitfire had returned.

Chapter Thirty

Char

He was going to suck it up whether he liked it or not. People did things because they cared and for no other reason. I cared. More than I should, judging by the hostile glances I kept receiving. He could be angry at me. I didn't care. What I did care about was keeping him occupied for the next few days. Jenny, a new nurse, had agreed to cover my shifts, while I tended to my outside patient.

Viper's mindset had taken on the victim mentality, and rightfully so, considering, but I needed to snap him out of it. Taking him home had been out of the equation. It would put him right back at the scene of his horrendous attempt at suicide. He needed a neutral space to help clear his head. Or that was my logic, anyway. I hope it worked.

I'd run it by Dec and he'd agreed. I had him on speed dial should I need him quickly.

I could feel the tension leaching out of Viper, so

the ride to Pinckney remained silent but tense. I wouldn't goad him any more than I already had. I needed to let him settle.

Pinckney hadn't changed and neither had the cabin if it could be called that. It resembled more of a lake house. Low set. White with blue shutters. Lots of deciduous trees surrounding the property. My folks hadn't been here in a couple of years, as they now lived in Maine, but I'd always had a key. I needed to utilize it more for relaxation time. It was kept well maintained by a local crew my father kept on salary.

Pulling in to the driveway and pressing the garage remote, I turned slightly to gage Viper's reaction.

His jaw remained firmly set and his focus, straight ahead. He'd be a tough nut to crack, but I never backed down from a challenge.

Turning off the ignition, I stepped out and moved to retrieve his bag and mine from the backseat.

Viper remained in the passenger seat.

"Do you need a hand getting out?" He had his crutches with him, so I knew he could probably do it, but it was in my nature to ask through concern.

Forcing open his door, he ignored my question, juggling himself and his crutches around so as to lever himself up. Slamming the door shut, he barked out, "Don't think I'm happy about this! You didn't even ask. You drove me to some hick town without my consent. So you've not only kidnapped me, you're holding me here against my will!"

God, he could be a dick. "Ha! First, I didn't force

you! I didn't hold a gun to your head…" Immediately regretting my words, I watched his face turn red and his eyes go colder. Gripping the crutches, he used the sudden adrenalin to surge forward. I moved back, a sinking feeling clutching my chest.

"I'm sorry. I didn't mean…"

Too late. He crowded my space. Even injured, he was a force to be reckoned with.

"You think you fucking know what's best for me? Just because you're a nurse? Well, news flash, lady! You don't know shit! You don't know me, and you sure as hell don't know how I feel or what I'm going through!

Anger rose. It was true I didn't know what he'd endured, but I knew enough about how the brain worked after life-altering injuries. I knew he was an ungrateful jackass.

Taking a deep breath to help tamp my ire, I slowly said, "You're right. I don't know you or how you feel, but I care, okay? I want to be here for you. I want to help. And it's not because of my job, or that I feel obligated. Stop pushing me away!"

His chest heaved. Eyes on fire. He resembled more of the Viper I knew at that moment and it caused my libido to nearly catch alight.

A flicker of humanity showed itself and then disappeared before he rotated and made his way inside.

I still held both our bags, so I trudged in behind him, taking his bag into the master suite with the bathroom. I took the spare room. I figured it would be easier for him to have the facilities closer.

The place smelled musty after being shut up for so long, so I opened windows, letting the cool breeze flow through. Viper had plonked himself on the couch in a huff, so I decided to ignore him and proceed to find the takeout menu my folks normally kept stuck to the fridge. Sure enough, it still remained.

"What pizza do you like?" I called out.

"Get whatever you want. I'm not hungry," he gruffed.

Fine. Meatlovers and Hawaiian coming up. I bet once he smelled it, he'd change his mind.

***

The atmosphere didn't change. I set the pizzas on the coffee table and filled my plate, watching and waiting to see if Viper would cave into the temptation. Nope. His strong will held firm, so I ate and placed the leftovers in the fridge, heading out back to sit on the verandah to watch the stars.

"Come out back with me? It's a gorgeous night."

He didn't even look at me, simply rose, and hobbled down the hallway to his room, slamming the door.

Would he keep this up the whole time? It was possible. Viper didn't do anything he didn't want to. I imagined he did really want the pizza, and would normally have sat outside with me, but his pride and stubbornness wouldn't give me the satisfaction.

Too bad, because the stars were extra bright, even with the bite in the air.

Pulling my cell out of my pocket once I'd settled

on the outdoor lounge chair, I dialed Mac.

"Hey, girl," she answered on the fourth ring.

"Hey."

"How's it going? You made it there okay?"

"Yeah. Just sitting out back, relaxing."

"How's Viper?"

"He's in his room, being an ass."

Mac chuckled. She knew the bantering that went on between His Highness and me. "You've got your work cut out for you. How will you cope over the next few days?"

"Honestly, I'm not sure. He wouldn't eat dinner. Wouldn't come sit out the back. He's actually really pissed I brought him out here."

"Hahaha. That sounds like him. You want a word with Dec to see if he knows how to break through the barrier Viper's put up?"

I wasn't sure his best friend had the answers either, but it was worth a shot.

Waiting for a minute, I heard shuffling and then a deep voice. "Char. What's up?"

His voice held mild concern.

"Nothing bad, just the usual. A stubborn, grumpy soldier to contend with. No biggie."

"He giving you a hard time already?"

"Well, let's just say he feels like I've kidnapped him."

Dec roared with laughter. "Maybe he's more himself than we thought."

"I just don't know what to do to help him. I thought he might like the idea of getting away from it all for a few days. Maybe it's just me he doesn't want to be around."

We'd had a weird relationship if you could call it that. It had so many bends and sharp corners to it, I couldn't keep up.

"I think you just need to toughen up some and tell him how it's gonna be. Don't let him walk all over you and be a dick. Get him outside tomorrow any way you can. He needs it. He's not going to sulk in his room forever. If I was there, I'd be on his ass like some drill sergeant, demanding he get his butt outside and moving. The longer he sits around feeling sorry for himself, the harder it will be to get him to do anything. You need me to come out there and kick his ass?"

Giggling, I replied, "No. Thank you. I just need to grow some balls and hope he listens to me. I'll give him tonight to sulk, but in the morning, I'll try what you said. He can only curse me and throw a tantrum, right?"

"Ahh, yeah. He probably will, but don't listen. Dig your heels in. Be tough with him. Don't take his crap. This is like an intervention. We're his friends and love him. We're doing this to help him. He may not see it, but eventually, he will. We're all he has. Seeing him with the gun to his head…"

He didn't finish. He didn't need to. "I'll handle it. Don't worry. I'll put my suit of armor on in the morning and become the bitch from hell."

"Atta girl. You got this. If taking the hardball approach doesn't work, then I don't know what will. Keep us posted, okay?"

"I will. And thanks. I mean it."

"All good."

After hanging up, I felt a little better. Maybe I

did need to harden up when it came to Viper. Show him I wasn't backing down or walking away, no matter what. Come morning, he was going to truly know the meaning of the term, *fiery redhead*.

Chapter Thirty-One

Char

Morning came and with it, life outside stirred. As for inside the house, silence ensued. Today was the day to test both of our wills. Sleep had come in fits and bursts. On and off. My mind had been on Dec's words. Toughen up. Don't take his crap. Could I do it? I'd like to believe so because if I failed, I'd be handing him over to his best friend. I'd never dealt with anything like it, personally. At work, we sent patients to therapy. An expert. Today, I needed to be that therapy. I hoped and prayed Dec knew his friend as well as he said he did.

Rising, I showered and made a pot of coffee, steeling myself for the morning ahead.

The lake house set back from the road in a thicket of trees that expanded down to the water. A track had been carved out by my father years ago, but with the caretakers focusing on only on the grounds around the house, everything had probably flourished.

We'd have to forge our own path. Kind of like life, really. This new road I traveled. I didn't have a clue what I was doing, but with one foot in front of the other, I'd discover new ground.

It was early. Seven thirty, to be exact. The sun was only beginning to raise its head. The sky had lightened, but the trees held the rays at bay.

Taking a long swig of coffee, I strode with purpose to the last room on the left. I didn't bother knocking, but blew in like a tornado, finding Viper asleep on his back with one arm covering his eyes. For a second, I faltered and just stared. Blankets covered his chest with only his head sticking out. October in Michigan was pretty cool. It felt like five degrees. I wore socks, sweats, and a long sleeve tee, but I knew in order to step outside, I'd need a jacket.

Viper's arms were bare, so I assumed he slept without a shirt, even in fall temperatures.

Dragging in a deep breath at his rugged handsomeness, I swallowed any doubts and moved forward.

"Rise and shine! Time to wake up and head outside!" My voice echoed in the quiet.

Viper stirred and turned slightly, but didn't wake. I neared the bed and jiggled him on the shoulder with my hand.

"Time to wake, Viper! The sun's up. You should be too." It sounded weird to be demanding he get up when technically he didn't have to. We didn't have anything to do other than making it to the lake, but if I was to let him know I was serious in my endeavor to help him, I needed to push aside any emotion and give him some tough love.

Both of his eyes opened and in a second were focused on me. Even bleary from sleep, they shot adrenalin into my bloodstream and upped my heart rate.

Don't back down, Char. You got this. Don't let him intimidate you. Stick to the plan.

"What the fuck are you doing?" he rasped, his brow scrunched up.

"Getting you out of bed. I didn't bring you out here to sleep all day. Get. Up!"

Shit. His face morphed into one of carefully controlled anger. I'd seen that look before and it scared the hell out of me. My brain yelled at me to back out of the room slowly and shut the door, but if I did that, I'd be giving in to him. I wouldn't follow through with it.

The sheets got thrown back, revealing his naked chest in all its masculine finery. My eyes wavered on the dips of his abdomen and then flew to his eyes as he pivoted to sit on the edge of the bed. His crutches stood against the wall beside the bed. Within reach.

An inferno blazed in the depths of such glorious green eyes.

"You think you can tell me what to do? Sorry to disappoint you, Red, but I'm not doing squat today, so I suggest you get that pretty ass out of here and go to the lake yourself."

He creaked his neck as if meaning business, and I'm sure he did. So much for taking charge. I needed to up my game.

Grounding both feet into the timber floor, I

gritted my teeth. "No! I'm not going alone." Needing to change tactics, I almost yelled, *I didn't peg you for a quitter. But that's exactly what you are. The going gets tough and you, what? Give up? Just like that!* Huffing, I placed a hand on my hip. "You disappoint me."

It killed me to say it. But I turned and stormed out of his room to the kitchen to finish the rest of my coffee. If he'd been one hundred percent mobile, there's no way I would have said what I did. I'd pay for it, but I couldn't dwell on that. The words were out. I heard a thud, followed by a loud, "Fucking bitch!"

Oh, I was in trouble all right. Scouring the kitchen, I pondered grabbing a weapon in self-defense. He sounded murderous as heavy clomping from the crutches pounded the hallway.

I hurried to the door leading outside and opened it so I could quickly escape, should I need to.

When Viper rounded the corner, the devil himself appeared. Every morsel of his boxer-clad body was squeezed tightly, ready to pounce.

"What the Goddamn hell did you say to me? Huh? I disappoint you? Is that what I do?"

Suddenly wishing I could take the words back, I held my breath. Part fear. Part anticipation. He was out of bed. I'd achieved that, but not in the way I'd wanted. I wanted him to come willingly.

He didn't disappoint me. Not by a long shot. But I'd said what I needed to. It had worked to an extent. Now, I didn't know what to do next.

Lifting my chin, I mock-laughed. "Your character disappoints me. I thought you were made of steel. Unbendable. Unbreakable. It would appear I was mistaken."

He took a step forward, then stopped. His face dropped slightly but recovered. My words had affected him. He tried hard not to show it, but I'd seen. Good. Maybe I could do this.

"Coffee's there. Help yourself to a cup."

Pointing to the machine, without glancing away, I noticed he didn't even blink, let alone follow my hand. I could only read his thoughts by the small tidbits he gave away via his face or body language. His white knuckles gripped his crutches desperately. His black irises had expanded, which I knew meant one thing. He was weighing up whether to strike or not.

"You think I can't handle anything you ask of me? I don't want to go outside. I don't feel like going to the lake. But you know what? Just to prove your sorry ass wrong, hold five. I'll fucking give you what you want. And when I make it to the lake? Then what? Are you going to gloat and say, "I told you so?""

"No. I'd never do that."

His eyes flashed as he pivoted around and began moving toward the hallway. "Fine. One trip to the lake and then you'll get off my case and I'll be free to do what I please until you get me the hell out of Dodge."

Victory. I'd done it. I didn't care if he sat inside every day hereafter. I'd touched a piece of his pride that wanted to prove me wrong. I didn't care about his pride. I only cared about reaching him.

I stepped out onto the back porch, shivering at

the fresh morning. Fingers crossed, the path to the lake wouldn't be too tricky to maneuver on crutches.

I wanted to cave to Viper's distress and coddle him, but not after my small victory. I'd push him further until we arrived back at the house later on. Then I'd let my wall of armor down and show him my compassion.

Five minutes exactly, the sliding door opened and Viper stepped out wearing sweats like me and a black tank. He obviously didn't feel the cold as much.

Slamming the door and giving me a glare which could ignite dry wood, he held out one hand as if gesturing me to lead the way.

Starting off, I turned to make sure he followed. His arms strained with the effort. His mouth held firm as he stared past me.

"If I injure myself further, I'm holding you fully accountable!" he growled.

I didn't answer. I hoped he didn't fall or have an accident and get hurt any worse. I couldn't live with that.

I kept a slow pace so he could keep up as we moved into thicker brush. Birds chirped and a slight breeze tickled the tops of the trees.

I found the path my father had created to be non-existent, so I forged a new route where there were fewer bushes and trees.

Every now and then I'd peer back to see if Viper was with me. He'd slowed somewhat, but he was still in view. I stopped to let him catch up.

When he caught me staring at him, he roared,

"Get an eyeful, Red? Are you frigging happy now? You got me outside. I'm moving. I'm doing it. I knew I could, but you obviously weren't as convinced I could do it."

"You're doing great."

He merely huffed and shook his head.

Large tree roots slithered across our virgin trail, so when I'd stepped over them, I called back to Viper. "Be careful of the roots. Take your time."

He didn't answer. Nor did I expect him to. I stood back and waited for his approach. A slight sheen of sweat had broken out on his skin, causing him to shine. With the dappled light of the sunrise through the trees, he appeared god-like. His half-leg didn't bother me at all. I had accepted it and looked beyond the missing limb.

"You expect me to get over that?" he asked, stopping.

"Yes, I do. Like I said, do it slowly."

He eyed me with suspicion. "What are you getting out of this? Why are you doing it?"

Did he mean the walk or standing by him in general?

Before I could say another word, he mumbled. "Forget it. You're insane. That's why you're making me do this."

He got over the first large root and took a shot at the next one, almost making it when his foot caught the top of it, putting him off balance. He tried to over-correct with the crutches but failed. I reached out as if from my distance I might be able to grab him, but I wasn't close enough. Watching in horror, he went down hard. Face down, over the last two tendrils of the tree's roots. Shit!

I moved without thinking. "Are you all right?" Silly question.

His face lifted with dirt on it. He'd let go of his crutches by putting out his hands to try and cushion his fall. I went to grab one, but a large hand came around my ankle, squeezing like a manacle. I sucked in a breath at the surprise move, stopping short just shy of his head.

"You!" he screamed. "You did this! You and your fucked up ideas! You see? Do you see now why this was a stupid, stupid plan? Look at me! Look. At. Me. This is disappointment, plain and simple. I'm disappointed in myself! I'll never walk properly again! Imprint this moment into your brain, sweetheart, because this is the new version of me. This is reality. Not some fantasy you've concocted in your head about life moving on as if nothing has happened." I'd never heard him so angry.

I felt terrible. I had caused this. Maybe Dec's plan hadn't been thought through enough. After all, not much time had passed since his return from Germany. In fact, it seemed so silly now that I'd even brought him to the lake house. He should have been at home recuperating. His psychologist had agreed to my request at bringing him out here, but perhaps we'd all got it wrong.

I dithered. He fumed.

"Get the fuck away from me. Leave me alone. You. Can't. Fix. Me. I'll find my own way back. And when I do, I'm calling a cab and heading home."

When I simply stood staring, eyes wide, he added, "Go! Get out of my sight."

His malice had me moving back, tears forming. I'd failed. I'd truly failed. He'd been right all along. It had been stupid to think he could overcome his disability so fast. It was even stupider to think I'd help make a difference.

He needed to cool down and I needed to get out of his orbit.

Spinning on my heels, I pushed through some leaves and branches blocking my way until I couldn't see him. I shouldn't be leaving him alone, but damn that man. He'd never accept my help now. How had I failed?

Dec's words kept playing over and over. He'd be disappointed. Now it would all be up to him to get through to his friend.

Get him outside any way you can. Dig your heels in.

Had I dug hard enough? I bet he'd listen to his military superiors if they were here. I bet he'd always taken orders from them.

My legs moved on their own as I played scenarios out in my head. Were there women in the military who men took seriously? How did they get their orders across?

Something triggered in my brain. A small spark of hope. I'd need to go all out and be someone I wasn't. Getting him out of the house had been a case of goading him. Making him want to prove me wrong. Could I do it again? Could I turn into a full-on drill sergeant?

I was almost at the lake. I could see water

twinkling through the trees. I should have kept going to sit for a bit, but the sliver of an idea I had begun to grow. As I remembered Viper's anger toward me at trying to help, my own blood began to boil. How dare he treat me like that! Sure, it may have been my fault that he was outside, but I didn't trip him up. He'd looked at me as if I was the vilest creature on the Earth.

Nope. I wasn't leaving him to stew while on his way back to the house to call a cab. I needed to fix things.

Reversing my journey, my feet stomped as my own anger fueled.

Finding him sitting against a tree with his head down, I moved into his space, deciding if I was going to be someone I wasn't, it needed to sound convincing.

"Eyes up, soldier!" I yelled at point blank range.

His head shot up, eyes drilling a hole through mine.

"What?" he gritted out, in my face.

Don't back down. Don't back down.

"I said, eyes up, soldier! On your feet! Now!"

I didn't recognize the woman barking orders. Surprise lit Viper's face for a moment so I urged on.

"That's an order! We don't give up. Ever. We're almost there. Do I have to carry you?"

I didn't move my face away from him or my penetrating stare. His eyes flickered and he blinked a couple of times, almost looking through me.

"Are you a quitter?" I screamed, my breath fanning over his skin. My voice was deafening but he didn't flinch. He didn't move. He sat stock still. I could tell his mind ticked over as he watched me.

"Answer me, soldier! Are you a quitter?"

A slight shake of his head.

Not good enough. "Answer me!" My throat had dried and began smarting with the force I used to propel my voice. I prayed to God this worked. Silence had me doubting, but holding my aggressive stance, eyeballing him, I watched as a shift took place.

"No, Sarge!" he roared back.

Not allowing myself a high-five yet, I got into the role.

"Then, I'm giving you an order! On your feet!"

Giving him some room, I stood, still unable to disengage my attention.

He paused, but slowly began to hoist himself up, using the tree trunk to lean into as he placed his crutches under his arms.

Finally!

"Now, move!" I hollered. "Don't be a pussy! Get your ass down to that lake at all costs! The enemy is on our tail!"

I could tell the moment he took on the true role of a soldier. His gaze turned from pissed at me to determined. He scoured the area as if a gun-wielding enemy might appear out of thin air. He'd jumped into the role, actually believing I was his sergeant. Another switch flicked. He had so many trigger points. He could go from one to the other in the blink of an eye. I'd just triggered the most significant one. Dec had been right. It was what he needed. I could see it in the sudden change in his posture. In the set of his mouth. His energy changed.

Roaring into the quiet, he pushed past me, and made it over the tree roots, vanishing into the brush before my eyes.

Not wanting to lose him, I kept pace, wondering how long I'd need to keep up the charade. Did he literally think he was back on tour?

What if I'd totally messed with his mind and turned him into someone with a split personality?

Ugh. I'd deal with that later. Right now I had to play out the role and see where it led. At all costs. I was truly winging it now and didn't know when or if I could stop.

His mighty warrior frame stood at the water's edge as I broke through the clearing. His upper torso heaved. He didn't turn when I approached.

Should I bark some more orders? We'd arrived at the lake. Now what? My adrenalin had peaked and was dropping.

I let him have a moment before touching his arm. It prompted him to whimper.

"Are you okay?" I asked, cautiously.

His head fell forward and his shoulders shook. Damn. Was he crying?

I edged around to the front of him, placing both my hands on his shoulders and pushing him more upright.

His head raised and my heart stalled. Fat sobs broke free as his tears fell. Pain. So much pain coated his features. Whatever false reality he'd been in moments earlier, he'd broken free of it.

"I'm sorry. I didn't mean to yell at you." Reality came crashing into me hard.

Never before had I taken such a tone with anyone, let alone a man. And least of all one who'd endured so much. Remorse flooded me.

He opened his mouth but nothing came out. I faced the water, ashamed I'd made a grown man cry. We stood in silence for way too long but I couldn't speak. I needed to know what went on in his brain.

"I…I didn't think I'd get to feel that again."

Confused, I faced him again. "What?"

"The thrill. The adrenalin surge. Knowing you're close to someone who will kill you as quickly as you could blink. Using the discipline of your superiors to do the best. To be the best. Using the part of your brain wired for war…" He choked on a sob. "For a brief moment, I was back there. I felt it."

All of a sudden, I got it. I got how his mind worked. A soldier's head lived and breathed in a different world to the one civilians existed in. We feared danger. Warriors like Viper craved it. He didn't know how to cope without it. He was afraid.

His attempted suicide. He probably didn't want to die, but he didn't want to live in a world without the rigid structure he had become so used to. He didn't do mundane and routine. Without the thrill of battle, he didn't know who he was. He was scared he'd totally lose himself back in the real world now that going on missions was no longer an option.

I didn't know how I'd ever replace the life he'd known. I couldn't.

"But you!" A tear fell onto his kissable lips. Lips I'd tried not looking at since arriving at the cabin. I couldn't help it now. The droplet held firm on his bottom lip until dropping off when he spoke again. "You feisty, frustrating, fucking amazing woman who I want to beat the crap out of right now."

Okay, now I was confused. Finding his red, watery eyes, I raised an eyebrow in question.

Steadying himself on his crutches, he raised his hand and placed it on my jawline. Palm flat. His thumb touched the corner of my mouth.

His touch lit my skin with goosebumps, the tenderness in stark contrast to the rest of him.

"You get it. You get me! You finally realize how I operate. I didn't think you ever would or could. Dec's the only one who understands. How did you figure out what I needed? What I still need?"

Should I let him in on Dec's helping hand? I didn't see why not.

"You shouldn't give me all the credit. Dec told me to play hardball. He didn't exactly tell me to go all military on you. That was all me."

He smiled. Actually smiled. An expression I'd missed so much. His whole face shone even with the tears.

"You fucking broke me wide apart, woman."

His grip tightened and he pulled me forward. I went willingly.

When his lips touched mine, I held on, supporting him at the same time. Both of his crutches dropped as his arms came around me. As the kiss deepened, my knees weakened but we held each other up.

I knew at that moment that I could do anything. Take on the world. I could be what Viper needed.

Pulling back, he asked, "The question is, are you willing to put me back together?"

Challenge accepted. I'd found my place in life. It was right here with this man whom I loved to hate. I had seen him at his worst and now knew how he ticked. With that knowledge, I could help him cope. If he needed me all badass and aggressive, I'd be what he needed. In return, he'd protect me, steadfast and true. He'd provide my body with what it needed and challenge me at every turn. But with his arms around me and his stunning green eyes showing me every emotion he could muster, I knew we were in this together. For the long haul. I wasn't a quitter and I'd damn well make sure he wasn't either.

Kissing him chastely, I replied, "Every last delectable piece. Now take me to bed. That's an order, soldier! Think you can make it back the way we came?"

He'd already let go of me and was crouching to pick up his ticket out of the woods.

Giving me a sideways, sexy smirk, his tears now drying, he led the way. "See if you can keep up!"

Everything would be all right. I tapped into the part of him he thought he'd never see again. He'd already lost his leg. Losing a piece of his soul had been a burden he hadn't wanted to carry. With me by his side, I'd take some of that load and lessen the burden. He understood now. Following behind him, he veered off the path we'd created on the way to the lake. For whatever reason, he'd changed, a new path formed. One with uncertainty but one he was willing to take. With me.

THE END

Acknowledgements

Thank you to Limitless Publishing for allowing me to publish my stories and reach thousands of new readers. It has opened up so many new doors for me that I never imagined possible and I've met the most amazing people!

Toni Rakestraw, my editor, you rock! My books shine with your dedication and support. I couldn't imagine putting my books into anyone else's hands. You see things I can't and have taught me a lot about writing and bettering my work. Thank you so much!

My friends and family. You guys are the best and I love you all. I wouldn't be who I am or where I am today without your unwavering support.

Chris Shramm! Thanks for helping me figure out a war scene I was having difficulty with. Having served in the army, there's no one I would trust more with firsthand knowledge about the subject.

Cher Shramm for always supporting my writing. We might not see as much of each other as I'd like, but you're still one of my best friends. Your strength continues to amaze me!

My housemate Audrey for letting me run scenes by you and giving me advice on something I'm stuck on. Thank you for being there for me during my stressful twelve months!

My readers for taking a gamble on my books and enjoying them. You are the reason I haven't given up. It's not an easy road being an author, and at times it's a lonely one, but getting positive feedback from even one person makes the journey worthwhile.

About the Author

I am married and a mother of two beautiful children, living in sunny Queensland, Australia. I've been reading books ever since I can remember and love all things related to books. Writing has become an extension of that and I hope to pursue a full time writing career. I currently write part-time and work as a remedial massage therapist. I love spending time with family and hope to one day travel to Italy and England.

Facebook:
https://www.facebook.com/amandamackeyauthorpage

Twitter:
https://twitter.com/AmandaMacey43

Website:
http://amandamackeyauthor.com/

Goodreads:
https://www.goodreads.com/author/show/7069947.Amanda_Mackey

www.ingramcontent.com/pod-product-compliance
Lightning Source LLC
Chambersburg PA
CBHW030614120726
47904CB00006B/1888